DOCTOR · WHO

T ARKSMITH LEGACY

BBC CHILDREN'S BOOKS
Published by the Penguin Group
Penguin Books Ltd, 80 Strand, London, WC2R 0RL, England
Penguin Group (USA) Inc., 375 Hudson Street, New York 10014, USA
Penguin Books (Australia) Ltd, 250 Camberwell Road, Camberwell, Victoria 3124, Australia
(A division of Pearson Australia Group Pty Ltd)
Canada, India, New Zealand, South Africa
Published by BBC Children's Books, 2009

Written by Richard Dungworth
Cover illustration by Peter McKinstry
10 9 8 7 6 5 4 3 2 1

ISBN: 978-1-40590-515-2
Printed in Great Britain by Clays Ltd, St Ives plc

DOCTOR · WHO

THE DARKSMITH LEGACY

THE COLOUR OF DARKNESS

BY RICHARD DUNGWORTH

The Darksmith adventure continues online. Log on to the website, enter the special codes from your book and enjoy games and exclusive content about *The Darksmith Legacy.*

www.thedarksmithlegacy.com

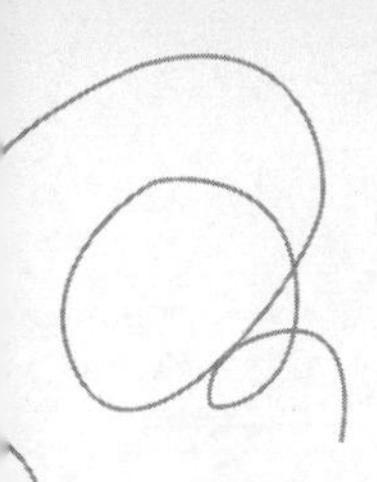

Contents

The Story So Far...

The Doctor has found the powerful Eternity Crystal, which was stolen from the Darksmith Collective by the Darksmith who created it – Brother Varlos. The Crystal has the power to bring dead matter back to life – like the corpses buried on the cemetery planet of Mordane. The Doctor knows the Crystal is so powerful it must be destroyed.

But the Darksmiths send a robot Agent to recover the Crystal. When the Doctor is forced to use the Crystal to save himself and his friends on Mordane, the Agent finds it, and returns it to the Darksmiths on their forbidding planet of Karagula...

A Price To Pay

The Doctor was used to running. Usually he was running *from* things, often angry, deadly things but right now he was running *to* something – the TARDIS. The disappearance of the Crystal had shocked him but there was only one possible explanation. The robot Agent had escaped from the catacombs and taken the Crystal.

The Doctor forced himself to keep running at top speed. Finally with his lungs bursting and both hearts pumping like crazy he reached the TARDIS. Quickly he unlocked the door and stumbled in on his aching legs. He hurried to the console and activated the scanners.

'Come on, come on, you can do it,' he muttered trying to encourage the TARDIS' systems to do the impossible but it was no good. There was no trace of the robot Agent or the Crystal's strange emissions on Mordane. The Agent and the Crystal had vanished completely.

The Doctor knew that the Crystal was dangerous. Too dangerous to be left with the Darksmiths. There was only one thing he could do.

The Doctor swallowed. There weren't many places in the Universe that frightened him but Karagula, home of the Darksmith Collective was one of them. Even when the Time Lords had been able to go to places in force they had never approached Karagula. Now he was the last of the Time Lords and he would have to face the Darksmiths alone.

His face dark with shadows, the Doctor entered the co-ordinates into the TARDIS guidance systems. With a quick pump of the bicycle pump, a final adjustment to the temporal buffers and a thump on the spatial drift circuits with his rubber tipped mallet the Doctor pulled the dematerialisation lever and set his space and time craft in motion.

'Next stop Karagula,' he announced to no-one in particular. 'I just hope this will be a return trip...'

Fra' Vallir strode gratefully into the shade of the council hall's arching canopy. At this time of day, the glare of Karagula's twin suns was too intense to bear for more than a few minutes at a time. Even the short walk from his own canopied quarters had left the back of Vallir's neck prickling and his brain half-baked. Normally the entire village would rest through the midday burn. But today Vallir and the other councillors had business to conclude.

He stepped lightly onto the council hall's floating platform, and headed for the pair of beaten-out alloy panels that formed the double-doors of the assembly chamber. He paused for a moment in front of them, feeling anxiety swell in his stomach.

What outcome would this meeting with the witch-woman have? What would her price be? It had been foolish of the council not to have agreed on a fee before accepting her bizarre offer.

But then, thought Vallir, *not one of us believed for a moment that she could actually…*

Pushing the doors aside, he entered the assembly chamber. The other eleven councillors were already present, seated around the chamber's horseshoe-shaped table. Vallir made his way to his own chair, between those of the council secretary, Fra' Sagral, and the treasurer, Fra' Tramlor.

Sagral, whose dead wife has returned to him.

TARDIS Data Bank

Karagula

Karagula is the sole planet orbiting the remote binary star of Izjol. Its status as 'habitable' is unconfirmed, but it is reputed to be the home world of the fabled Darksmith Collective, an ancient guild of artisans whose origins and activities are shrouded in myth.

STELLAR DATA

Karagula's two suns – the companion stars Izjol A and Izjol B – are both G2 stars. This is the same classification as Earth's Sun. It means they have a surface temperature of around 5500°C, and a core temperature of around 15,600,000°C. At 4.5 billion years old, the Izjol stars are also of comparable age to the Sun.

ORBITAL PATH

For a planet orbiting a single star, such as Earth orbiting the Sun, the path of the planet is caused by the attraction between the two

bodies, known as gravitation. In a binary system like Izjol's, both stars exert a gravitational force. This makes Karagula's orbital path very complex.

SURFACE CLIMATE

Each of the Izjol stars can be assumed to have a similar energy output to the Sun – approximately 386 billion billion megawatts. The climate on Karagula, in close orbit around them, is therefore predicted to be hot and dry.

And Tramlor, whose daughter's sightless eyes now see. How can such things come to pass?

He sat, and gave a nod to an attendant standing at the chamber's side entrance. The clerk drew aside its scrap-mesh curtain and ushered in a young, dark-haired woman. She crossed to sit on the bench encircled by the council table.

During her previous visit to the council hall a few days ago, Vallir had been struck by the woman's unusual beauty. There was a rich, misty softness about her, almost as though one's eyes could not quite bring her into focus. She wore the same simple, pale blue robe and meek expression now as she had that day.

But Vallir's opinion of her was utterly changed. This woman had powers he could not comprehend. She was as dangerous as she was beautiful, he was sure. And the council was in her debt.

He cleared his throat.

'You seek an audience with us, madam?'

'Yes, Chief Councillor.' The woman's voice had a hypnotic lilt. 'I trust you are satisfied that I have fulfilled my part of our contract?'

Vallir shuffled awkwardly.

'You have done as you said you would. Though it

is beyond my understanding how you have brought about such impossibilities.'

'Then the time has come, I believe, for me to name a price for my services.'

'But within our means!' interjected a large, red-faced man to Vallir's left. 'It was clearly stated that your fee should be easily within our means!'

Vallir raised a hand for calm.

'Thank you, Fra' Callord.' He met the woman's cool gaze. 'As my fellow councillor points out, the price, though yours to name, must be one that we can comfortably afford – such was our agreement.'

'Indeed, Councillor.' She smiled archly. 'I can assure you that the payment I seek will leave your purses full. And I am glad you intend to keep your side of our bargain.' She absently fingered a small stone pendant that hung at her neck. 'I have friends who would be unhappy to see me swindled.'

Dark looks fell across the councillors' faces. It had been the pendant that had originally persuaded them not to dismiss the woman's absurd proposal. They had recognised the black flame design inlaid in the rough stone only too well. It was the sign of the Darksmiths. And a friend of theirs was not to be offended lightly.

Vallir fixed the woman with a firm stare.

'The integrity of this council is not in question. We made an agreement under Lithic Oath, and it will be honoured.'

'Very well. Then I shall name my price.' The woman paused, then continued matter-of-factly. 'Your children. My price is your children.'

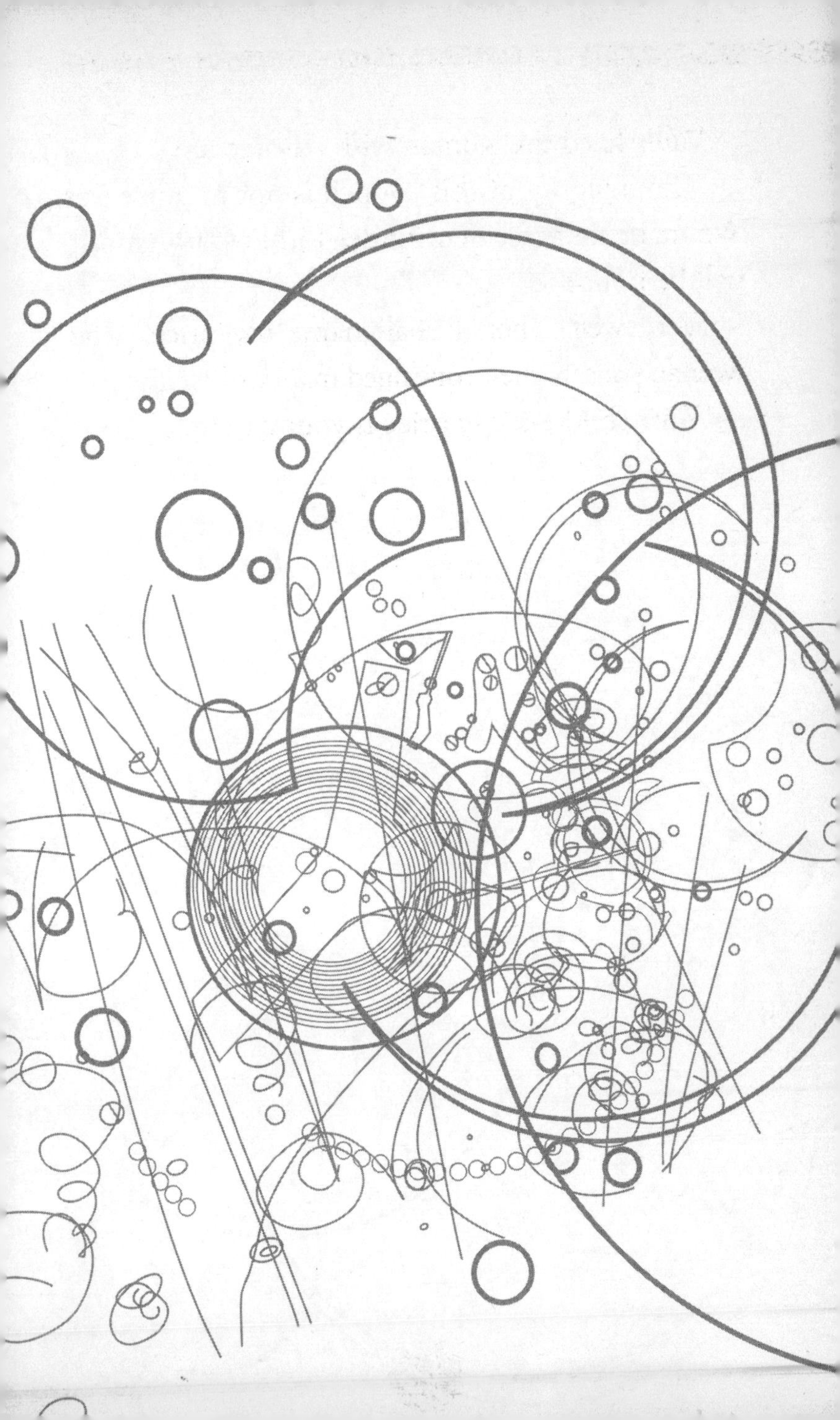

A Warm Welcome

'Blimey – that is *hot*!'

The Doctor wrestled off his suit jacket, and lobbed it casually through the open doors of the TARDIS behind him.

Screwing up his eyes against the glaring sunlight, he took several strides forward to where the rocky plateau, on which the TARDIS had materialised moments earlier, fell away in a sheer drop. He peered over the brink and raised an eyebrow.

'*Little* bit close for comfort. Probably ought to tweak the avoidance sensors a smidge. Still…' – he balanced precariously for a moment on one trainer-covered foot, dangling the other out into thin air – '… any materialisation you can walk away from..!'

Shielding his eyes with one hand, he scanned the unfamiliar landscape from his cliff-top viewpoint. It wasn't the *most* hostile environment he had ever encountered. That had to be the acid-spitting sulphur-fields of Gomrath's gas moons. Or possibly the Newt and Noggin juice bar on Alphura III. Nevertheless, the sun-scorched wasteland below him looked rather less than welcoming.

A dry, rocky plain stretched away as far as his dazzled eyes could see. Distant mountains formed a jagged horizon. And above it all, the planet's twin suns burned mercilessly in a pale, sickly sky.

'I can see the brochure now,' muttered the Doctor. '"Come to craggy old Karagula." Perhaps it's nicer in the not-quite-so-insanely-hot season.' He could only hope the hunch that had brought him to this dreary, dried-up planet proved correct. This *had* to be where the Agent had brought the Crystal, didn't it? Back home. To the planet of its creators – the Darksmith Collective, of whom the robotic Agent had spoken so reverently.

Something caught the Doctor's eye. A faint dust-cloud hung over one area of the plain below. Beneath it, he could see a cluster of pale, sail-like shapes, each angled to reflect the glare of the sun. The smaller ones were huddled around a giant central umbrella-shaped canopy. In the shade it cast, the Doctor could just make out a structure of some kind.

'Signs of life. Time to get down there and meet the locals.'

The Doctor's wish was fulfilled sooner than expected. He turned back from the cliff-edge to find five humanoid figures standing silently in a semi-circle around him.

Humanoid, but not human, thought the Doctor. *You don't get humans with amber-coloured eyes.*

All five were male, dark-skinned. They had a thick yellow substance smeared across their cheeks, the bridges of their flat noses and the upper surfaces of their bare feet. And all were holding hunting spears, tipped with razor-sharp shards of black, glassy rock.

'Hello! Aren't you the stealthy ones. Didn't hear you at all. Well, not much. Well...' The Doctor stepped forward, hand outstretched. 'Anyway, I'm the Doctor.'

He immediately froze, as five lethal-looking spear tips jabbed to within centimetres of his throat.

'Ah. OK. Not *overly* keen on strangers, then. Fair enough.'

He smiled unthreateningly.

The men stared at him suspiciously, weapons

still raised. Beyond them, the Doctor could see two more figures pacing cautiously around the TARDIS. They were peering at it inquisitively, prodding at it now and then with their spears.

'This may all be new to you,' continued the Doctor, 'but it strikes me as a classic Take Me To Your Leader moment, don't you think? If you *have* a leader, of course. I mean, you don't seem the savage, leaderless type. Which is nice.'

He offered both upturned wrists, clearly indicating a willingness to have them bound.

'Not too tight, please. I like to keep the circulation going in my fingers.' He beamed broadly. 'I'm all yours!'

Bethin's head swam sickeningly as she teetered on the brink of consciousness. As her senses returned, her mind was suddenly flooded with information.

Her feet hurt. She was hot and terribly thirsty. Her neck stung. And she was moving, walking.

She opened her eyes, then screwed them tightly shut against the white-hot sunlight. A few seconds later, she tried again, lifting her eyelids more cautiously.

She was walking up a gentle rocky incline. No,

not walking – marching, marching in a group. As her eyes adjusted to the glare, she looked ahead, then behind her. She was among a host of about fifty children. They were plodding forward, in pairs. All had their eyes closed and blank expressions on their faces, as if they were sleepwalking.

Bethin spotted Tirril, her classmate, a few rows back. Fra' Jared's son, two years her junior, paced robotically beside her. In fact, the marching group seemed to include all the village children – although she couldn't see her brother anywhere among them.

Where are we going? Why are we out in the open?

All villagers were taught from a young age to avoid the unforgiving glare of their planet's suns. The yellow paste of Samal flowers would protect her face and feet a little. But in the height of day, Sun Fever could take you within minutes. A daylight hike beyond the protection of the village's canopies was madness.

Keen to see where they were destined, Bethin lifted her gaze beyond the head of the column of marching children. And her heart missed a beat.

Ahead, a massive building loomed up from the mountainside they were steadily climbing. Its towering walls were smooth and dark, supported by heavy buttresses of black rock. Bethin could make out hideous gargoyles leering down from below the arching stone roof. The whole structure looked as though it had been carved from the mountain itself.

Bethin's shock broke whatever spell was forcing her to continue her trance-like marching. She halted. As the other children filed past her, zombie-like, she stared up at the awesome edifice.

There was only one place this could be. The Dark Cathedral, of which the village adults spoke in hushed voices.

Suddenly, the other children came to a standstill. As one, each pair separated, creating a channel down the centre of their marching line. Bethin saw a figure approaching along it and immediately recognised the pale blue robe. It was the woman who had come to their village only days earlier.

As the woman approached, Bethin's mental image of her flickered strangely. The woman's figure became blurred, out of focus. For a split second, it was replaced by the image of a nightmarish creature – multi-limbed with vast, blackened eyes and reptilian scales.

An instant later, the vision passed. Bethin found

herself confronted by the blue-robed woman, who now gave her a wry smile.

'You're a feisty one, aren't you young lady? Few have the inner strength to override a Black Incense trance.'

Bethin continued to stare uncomprehendingly. Her voice refused to function.

'No matter. An extra dose will prevent you delaying our progress further.'

There was a faint hissing sound, and Bethin thought she briefly saw a dark vapour trail in the air. Then it was gone.

'Now – shall we press on?'

The woman turned, and began making her way back to the head of the column. Watching her, Bethin experienced another split-second vision of an encrusted back, and long, scaly tail.

As the woman passed, the other children fell back into their pairs behind her. In perfect synchronisation, they began to march again. Bethin felt panic rise inside her. Darkness was once again seeping across her mind like a black inkblot. She fought to stay awake, to drive the darkness back, but it was no use.

Her last conscious sensation was of her own legs once more falling into rhythmic strides…

On closer inspection, the settlement the Doctor had spotted from the cliff-top proved fascinating. As he was escorted through its outskirts – and into the welcome shade of the spreading, sail-like canopies that arched overhead – he marvelled at the peculiar dwellings scattered around him.

They were ramshackle cabins, each built from a wide variety of reclaimed materials; corrosion-pocked panels of sheet-metal, bits of carbon-fibre mesh, fragments of patched canvas. Each makeshift structure was mounted on a rough timber platform. It was these that caught the Doctor's imagination.

'They float! That's *marvellous.* Little houses bob-bob-bobbing along!'

He dropped down to peer beneath the nearest hovering platform's underside.

'And no sign of AntiGrav technology. How's that work, then? Some sort of inertia-avoidance system, is it?'

A firm spear-prod forced him to his feet, and onward. As his captors marched him further into the strange floating shantytown, the Doctor noticed larger platforms carrying neatly ordered agricultural plots. These were crammed with assorted vegetables, fruits and cereal crops, many of which he didn't recognise. Like the platforms bearing homes, these agri-platforms hovered half a metre above the planet's rocky surface.

And all the platforms were moving. Only a centimetre per second, perhaps, but moving nonetheless, drifting steadily along in the same direction.

The Doctor spotted an antique-looking magna-couple lashed to a nearby platform, invisibly linking it to its neighbour. Another coupling hitched this platform to a third. The entire settlement was clearly under tow, linked together like barges behind a tug.

'Moving house?' enthused the Doctor. 'Excellent!'

The Doctor's arrival seemed expected. On many of the floating platforms, men similar in appearance to his guards stood beside the entrances to their homes. They watched his progress with hostile glares. Their women-folk were with them, their dark faces decorated with the same thick yellow paste.

No youngsters though, thought the Doctor, unable to pick out a single child among the scowling onlookers. *That's odd.* 'Kids all at school, are they?' he asked.

The Doctor's query was met with a silence as stony as the landscape – like all his previous attempts to make conversation. Another prod in the back urged him forward towards a slightly larger cabin just ahead.

'Oh look at this. Posh-looking place like this has to belong to someone important. Am I right?'

He stepped nimbly up onto the hut's floating platform and felt it dip very slightly under his weight. Another spear jab goaded him through a flap of canvas in the cabin's front wall.

In the end, the Doctor's captors hadn't tied his hands, settling for keeping their weapons trained on him as they had escorted him from the cliff-top. So now, as he faced the tall, stern-looking man waiting inside the hut – a figure of some authority, judging by his robes and armed attendant – he once again offered his hand in greeting.

As before, the gesture provoked a warning spear thrust, this time from the guard at the man's side.

The Doctor hastily withdrew his hand, and squinted distractedly at the glassy black spear tip centimetres from his face.

'Nice spearhead. Carved from obsidian, I see. Good choice. Best thing for creating a blade. Molecular structure means it can be ground to a finer edge than almost anything else. You guys certainly know your rocks.'

'Stone-lore is central to the Karagulan way of life.' The robed man's voice was deep and rich. 'As you would know, were you native to this land.'

He gestured for the guard to lower his spear, but remained hard-faced.

'But your appearance suggests you are from other parts. The scout who was sent ahead to inform us of your capture spoke of your arrival in a strange blue craft...'

'The TARDIS. That's my sort of anti-gravity magic move-about thing. And I'd be really grateful if –'

'So you confess to being a trespasser on our territory?'

'Well, I prefer the term *traveller*. You see – '

'We do not welcome strangers to our village.'

The Doctor gave an ironic laugh.

'I'd sort of guessed. I'm unarmed. I was nice as pie to your friends outside. Yet I've had a spear shoved at me more times in the last hour than I care to remember! Don't get me wrong, but my idea of a warm welcome is more the cup-of-tea-and-a-biscuit kind of thing.'

The man's face flushed.

'In the past, we have extended hospitality and friendship to many guests. But such naivety has recently cost us dearly.' A sadness crossed his face. 'The deceptions of our last visitor have left our community desolate. If you find us suspicious, it is not without reason.'

The Doctor gave a nod of acknowledgement.

'Fair enough. Once bitten, twice shy, I suppose. But you needn't worry about *me*. Totally harmless. Well – *mostly*. Well, no sinister intent, anyway. Cross my hearts.'

The man held the Doctor's wide-eyed gaze silently for several seconds, as though trying to get the measure of him. Then he looked down awkwardly.

'I'm sorry. Until you have fully explained your sudden appearance and stated your business before the council, you must be held under lock and key. For the safety of the village. The council will determine your fate.'

He clapped his hands, and two of the Doctor's original guards ducked through the entrance.

'Take him away.'

As the Doctor was shepherded out, he glanced over his shoulder and flashed the man a friendly grin.

'No hard feelings. But see what you can do about that cup of tea, mm?'

High Minister Drakon stood on the gallery of the Dark Cathedral's cavernous entrance hall. He watched as the ranks of mesmerised children filed across the worn flagstones below.

Under his long hooded cloak, Drakon's form could easily have been mistaken for that of a human. But his hood shadowed a face that was wholly alien. His head was hairless. The bones of his skull were clearly visible through the tissue that covered them. Generations of living out of the light had left the Darksmiths of Karagula with little pigment in their flesh. They shared the eerie translucency of other creatures that burrowed deep into darkness, or swam in lightless ocean depths.

Drakon watched the woman in sky blue robes lead the children away along the blackness of one of the Cathedral's main corridors. He didn't approve of this Dreamspinner business. In the high days of the Collective, when Brother Varlos had still been with them, such petty dealings would have been scorned.

But since Varlos' betrayal, they had fallen on harder times. Drakon himself chose to have nothing to do with the Dreamspinner's strange concoctions. But he knew many of his Brothers and Sisters – even some of those in the Witan, the Darksmiths' ruling council, were growing increasingly dependent on them.

'High Minister!'

Drakon turned to greet a second cloaked figure. 'Brother Ardos – what news?'

'The Agent has returned, High Minister!'

'And the Crystal? Do you have the Eternity Crystal?'

Ardos looked a little uncomfortable.

'There is a slight problem, High Minister. The Agent *is* back on Karagula. But we have yet to actually retrieve it. The pod's re-entry systems malfunctioned. It crash-landed, High Minister. Communications have gone dead.'

Drakon scowled. Ardos hurriedly continued.

'But our probes on the surface are picking up clear traces of the Crystal. It's out there, High Minister. With the Agent, I'd guess. We just have to determine exactly *where*.'

Ardos pulled a thin, slate-like tablet of rock from under his cloak. He grasped its edges, and it expanded to the dimensions of a laptop screen. As Ardos tapped it with a translucent thumb, its surface lit up.

'According to our scanners, the pod's wreckage is located at the six sites shown here.' He pointed to the display. 'The Crystal must be at one of them. Our surface probes – marked A, B and C – are all picking up traces of it. The signal is stronger at Probe A than at Probe B, but strongest at Probe C.'

Drakon took the device impatiently from his fellow Darksmith.

'Which means the Crystal is at a wreckage site nearer to A than it is to B, but nearest to C,' he muttered, scrutinising the display.

A few seconds passed in silence. Then Drakon jabbed a finger at the display.

'Send a recovery party to this wreckage site immediately. They will find the Eternity Crystal there.'

He handed the display device back. 'Bring me the Crystal, Ardos.' Drakon's eyes burned with determination. 'Only when it has been safely recovered can the Darksmith Collective ascend to its former glory. The Crystal is everything!'

Activity

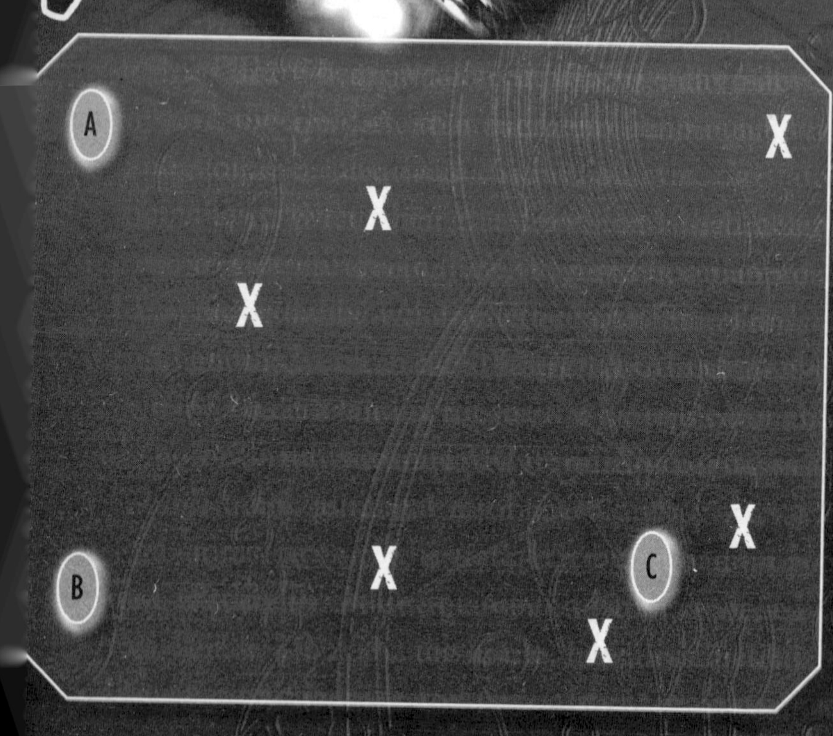

X = wreckage site ● = scanning probe

Which wreckage site is nearer to Probe A than it is to Probe B, but nearer to Probe C than it is to either A or B?

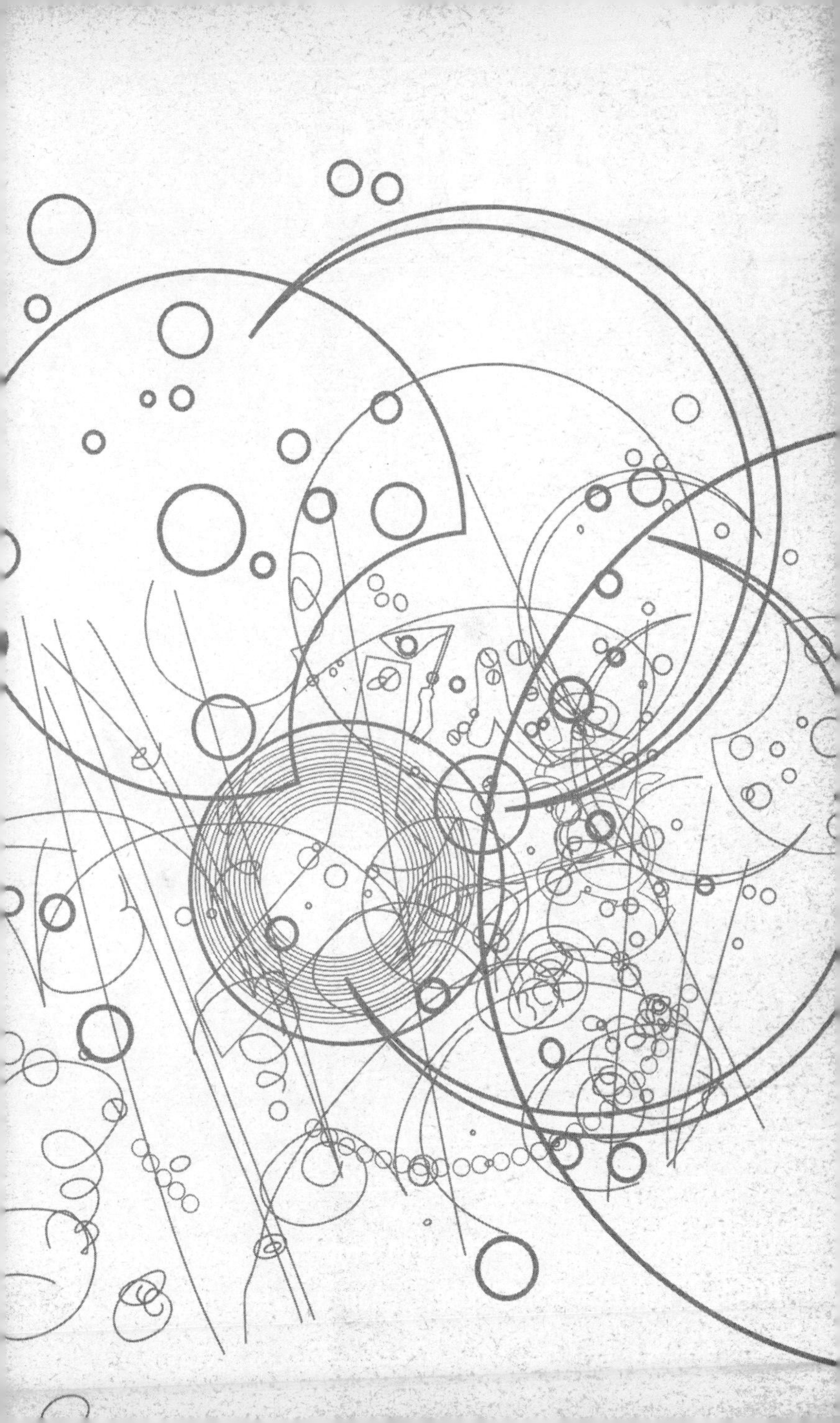

Lorton's Story

The Doctor's cell was a basic affair – a makeshift cage made from old metalert pallet-rods crudely welded together. This unusual community was clearly largely dependent on recycled junk.

Even so, without his sonic screwdriver, unfortunately tucked in his jacket pocket back in the TARDIS, the Doctor was having little luck trying to pick the door's heavy padlock.

He broke off his efforts at the sound of someone approaching, expecting to see one of the burly guards who had escorted him into this airless, swelteringly-hot cabin an hour or more ago.

To his surprise, it was a child – a boy of about ten years old.

'Hello! I hope you've brought ice creams. It's absolutely *roasting* in here.'

The boy eyed the Doctor warily through the barred cell door, then turned to where another cage stood against the cabin's opposite wall. On a rough bench inside this second cell lay an elderly, white-haired man. He had been sleeping soundly since the Doctor's arrival – despite the Doctor's best efforts to engage him in conversation. This was evidently who the child had come to see.

'A friend of yours? Boy, can he snore! Sounds like a Slitheen gargling...'

The boy turned. The Doctor grinned warmly. 'Don't worry – I won't bite! Just making conversation. I'm harmless, well mostly.'

The youngster spoke at last. 'Fra' Vallir mustn't think so, or he wouldn't have had you locked up.'

'Yeah, well from what I can gather, Fra' Vallir – he's the tall gloomy chap, yes? – thinks just about *everybody* is a threat.'

The boy seemed to acknowledge this. 'That's because of her.'

'*Her* who?'

'The travelling woman.' He glanced back at the man in the other cell, affection clear in his face. 'The one that Grandfather thought was a monster.'

'And this is your granddad? How come he's got

himself locked up in here?'

The boy turned back to the Doctor. 'When the travelling woman arrived in our village, Grandfather went crazy. Really hysterical, like he was mad with terror. He kept screaming and yelling about this horrible creature he could see. But when he pointed to where it was, he was pointing at the woman. It made no sense.'

'Has he had strange visions before?'

'No, never. My sister and I tried to calm him, but he just kept raving about the monster, and trying to drive the woman out of the village. In the end, the council decided he had to be locked up before someone got hurt. They've been giving him peace leaf – to keep him sedated.'

The Doctor saw anger flash in the boy's eyes.

'He was right, too,' the boy said. 'She *was* a monster.'

'The travelling woman?'

'She called herself a "Dreamspinner". Said she could "make our hearts' desires come true". Everyone thought it was a load of rubbish, of course. But the village Council made a deal with her. They said that if she could prove she really *could* make our dreams into reality, then she could name her fee.'

The Doctor nodded. 'Tell me.'

The boy frowned. 'And somehow – somehow I don't understand – she did it. Made people's wishes come true. She spent three days talking to everyone in turn. Then, when we woke on the fourth day, things had changed. Amazing things.'

'But at a cost, right?' the Doctor asked. He was beginning to get a bad feeling about this.

'Since the woman had done as she'd promised, the council said we had to pay whatever price she named. And she demanded the children – all of them. She rounded up every child in the village – my sister Bethin, my friends, all of them – and led them away.'

The Doctor was incredulous. 'But why didn't somebody stop her?'

The boy shrugged. 'I thought the grown-ups would stop it happening, or at least that the kids would put up a struggle. Beth's pretty tough when she wants to be. But it was like they were all in some kind of trance, or something. The kids did whatever the woman told them, and their parents just watched as she marched them away. That was over a week ago, and nobody's seen them since.'

'If she took all the other children, why not you?'

The boy's chin dropped a little.

'When they locked Grandfather up, I had a big row with Fra' Vallir. I ran away. Didn't last long though. Two days later they fetched me back in a sorry state. Sun Fever, and bad, too. On the day that the Dreamspinner took Beth and the others, I still wasn't fit to walk. They had to leave me behind.'

The Doctor's brow furrowed. 'Wish-granting is strictly fairytale stuff. It's not *real.* It doesn't actually work. Well, not usually. Not unless there's something very fishy going on. I think I need to have another chat with your Fra' Vallir.' He fixed the boy with an earnest look. 'What's your name?'

'Lorton.'

'Well, Lorton, I can help your sister. And your granddad. But not if I'm locked in here.'

The boy hesitated. He looked across at his sedated grandfather, then back to the Doctor. 'What do you want me to do?'

'Bravo! Bravissimo, in fact! What I need right now is something long and thin, to pick this padlock...'

Lorton hastily delved in his trouser pocket. He held out his palm to display a collection of miscellaneous bits and bobs. As he did so, something that looked like a small white pebble began to rise impossibly from his palm into thin air. It floated gently upwards, until the boy quickly snatched it with his other hand.

'What's that?' asked the Doctor, intrigued.

'Float-stone,' replied Lorton. 'It's made from Axite ore – you find little bits of it in rocks all over. If you fuse enough of it together, it floats. It's what they use to make the platforms hover.'

'Brilliant!' exclaimed the Doctor. 'It must be repelled by the planet's magnetic core…'

Lorton rooted through his remaining treasures and extracted a short length of thick wire. 'How about this? Any good?'

The Doctor gave him a broad grin. 'Just the job.'

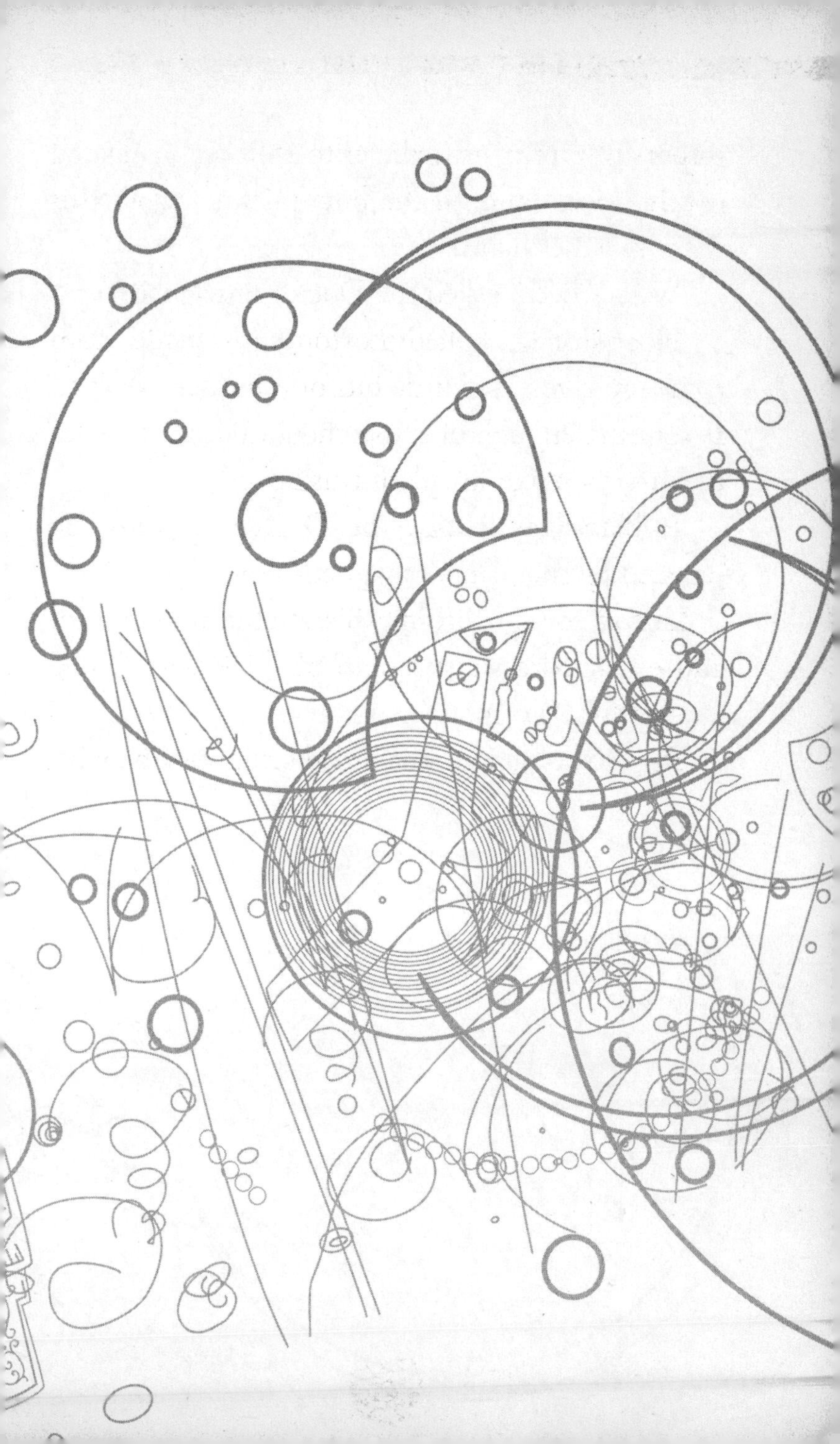

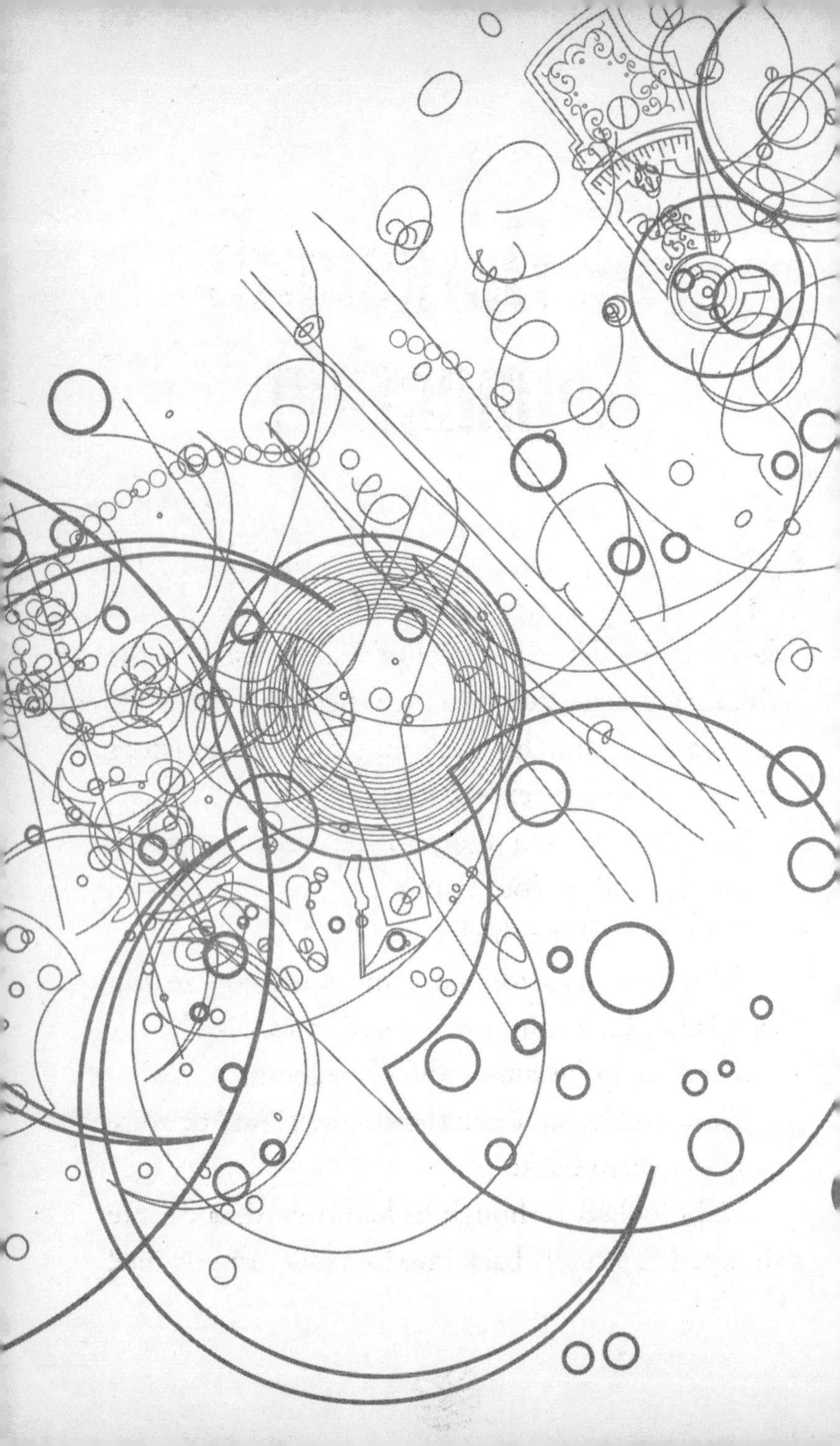

The Darksmith Connection

'So – tea ready yet, Fra' Vallir? Pot still warming, is it?'

If the Chief Councillor was alarmed by the Doctor's unexpected entrance, he hid it well. He rose calmly from his desk and met the Doctor's smile with a stony expression.

'You have me at a disadvantage, sir,' he growled. 'I am yet to learn your name.'

'You can call me the Doctor.'

'Very well, *Doctor*. Give me one good reason why I shouldn't summon a guard immediately.'

The Doctor became suddenly solemn.

'Because I know about the children. And because I can get them back.'

Vallir looked as though he had been slapped. He slumped dejectedly back into his chair. 'Impossible!

Believe me, there is nothing I desire more. My own son is among those taken by that cursed woman. But she made a legitimate claim. The council *had* to concede to her demand. We are bound to the foolish pact we made by Lithic Oath.'

'Not if you were duped,' replied the Doctor. 'Look, *nobody* has the power to make an entire village's dreams come true. Not the Tooth Fairy, not my Fairy Godmother, and not this "Dreamspinner" woman. It's a set up. You've been had. Tricked. Conned.'

'But the evidence is all around us,' insisted Vallir. 'The woman *did* make our wishes into reality! Take my fellow councillor Fra' Sagral – his wife died of Sun Fever four seasons ago. His heart's desire was to have her back and now she walks among us again. How do you explain *that*, Doctor? Or our smith, Fra' Ballord, whose crushed hand was restored?'

The Doctor wasn't deterred.

'The only way you could change current reality – bring someone back to life, or un-squish an injured hand – would be to travel back in time to alter the past events that shaped that reality. But you can't just tweak an individual's past to obtain a desired change in their present. Timelines inter-relate, cross, merge – it's a bit complicated. Timey-wimey.'

He leaned closer to the baffled councillor.

'But, what *is* possible – what is *just* possible – is to mess with someone's memory or their perception, so that they *think* their wishes have come true.'

Vallir still looked flummoxed. The Doctor ploughed on.

'What if Fra' Sagral's wife *didn't* die four seasons ago? Or your friend Ballord's hand was never crushed? What if those are *false* memories that this woman implanted in each villager's mind somehow. Through hypnosis, maybe. Then the reality that existed before she ever came along – that Mrs Sagral was alive and kicking, that Ballord had an unharmed hand – would seem like a dream come true.'

Fra' Vallir mulled this over for a moment.

'So you're suggesting that the woman changed nothing in our lives, but only altered our collective memory of our past so that we believed certain desirable details of our present were the results of her actions?'

'One big fat con trick. The secret to seeing through it is to dig deeper into your false memories. There's no way that she'll have been able to fill in the really nitty gritty itty-bitty details. Like – who went to Mrs Sagral's funeral, hmm? What did everyone eat afterwards? Was it as hot as it is today? Who said nice things, and who ate or drank too much?'

A clouded look came above Fra' Vallir's face.

'I… I… can't remember… now that you ask me, I have no recollection of a ceremony…'

The Doctor raised his eyebrows. 'Well, if your lady friend hasn't delivered what she claimed she would, then you're off the hook. What's the big deal with this Lithic Oath, anyway? I'm all for keeping promises, but I can't imagine any agreement so binding that you'd settle it with your own *children*!'

Fra' Vallir had looked briefly hopeful. Now his expression became solemn once more. 'The Lithic Oath – the Oath of Stone – is a bond upheld by a terrible authority. The Dreadbringers of the Darksmith Collective.'

'Ah!' The Doctor's eyes lit up. 'Now you've *really* got me interested. I've some unfinished business with the Darksmiths. I've heard the legends of course. I think I'm even *in* some of them. But who exactly *are* they? Really?'

'Their history is, in part, that of my own people,' said Fra' Vallir. 'When our ancestors first colonised this planet –'

'Lovely spot, too,' grinned the Doctor. 'Bit hot though.'

'– they found the ferocity of its suns too extreme to endure. Countless generations ago, Karagulans divided into two factions, each of which sought to find a way to survive the solar glare.

'The surface-dwellers developed a nomadic culture. We are constantly on the move, following a seasonal migration across our world that ensures we experience the minimum exposure to sunlight.'

'I get it. You chase the shortest day!'

'Exactly. By doing this, and by living mostly beneath our sun-canopies, we are able to survive.

'The other group – the Darksmiths – sought an alternative solution. They established a realm out of the sunlight altogether – beneath the planet's surface. Their civilisation did well, developing advanced technologies in the darkness, establishing trade-links with alien peoples. It survives today deep under the mountains, accessible only via its portal with the surface – the Dark Cathedral.'

'I've seen their advanced technology. Up close and personal. Nasty but impressive. Is that why you're so keen not to upset them?'

'In part. But there is a more critical reason. You have seen how we surface-dwellers are dependent on scrap materials for our buildings and technologies. Resources on this barren planet are scarce. What little materials we have – the ancient motors that propel our village, the reclaimed metalert struts that suspend our canopies – all come from the Darksmiths' scrap heaps. If we offend them, or those in alliance with them, our society's survival will be in jeopardy.'

Fra' Vallir's expression became grave once more. 'So, even if the Dreamspinner was a fraud,' he went on, 'I cannot see how we can challenge her. She wore a pendant that clearly showed her alliance with the Darksmiths. I suspect she came to us from the Dark Cathedral itself – at this point of our migration we pass nearer to it than at any other.'

The Doctor clapped his hands abruptly. 'Well, *your* hands might be tied, but I think I'll pay the Darksmiths a quick visit. I just need a couple of things from the TARDIS –'

'The blue box? I had it transported from the cliff-side. It is in our safe-keeping – '

'– then it's time someone shed a little light on the affairs of your Darksmith cousins…'

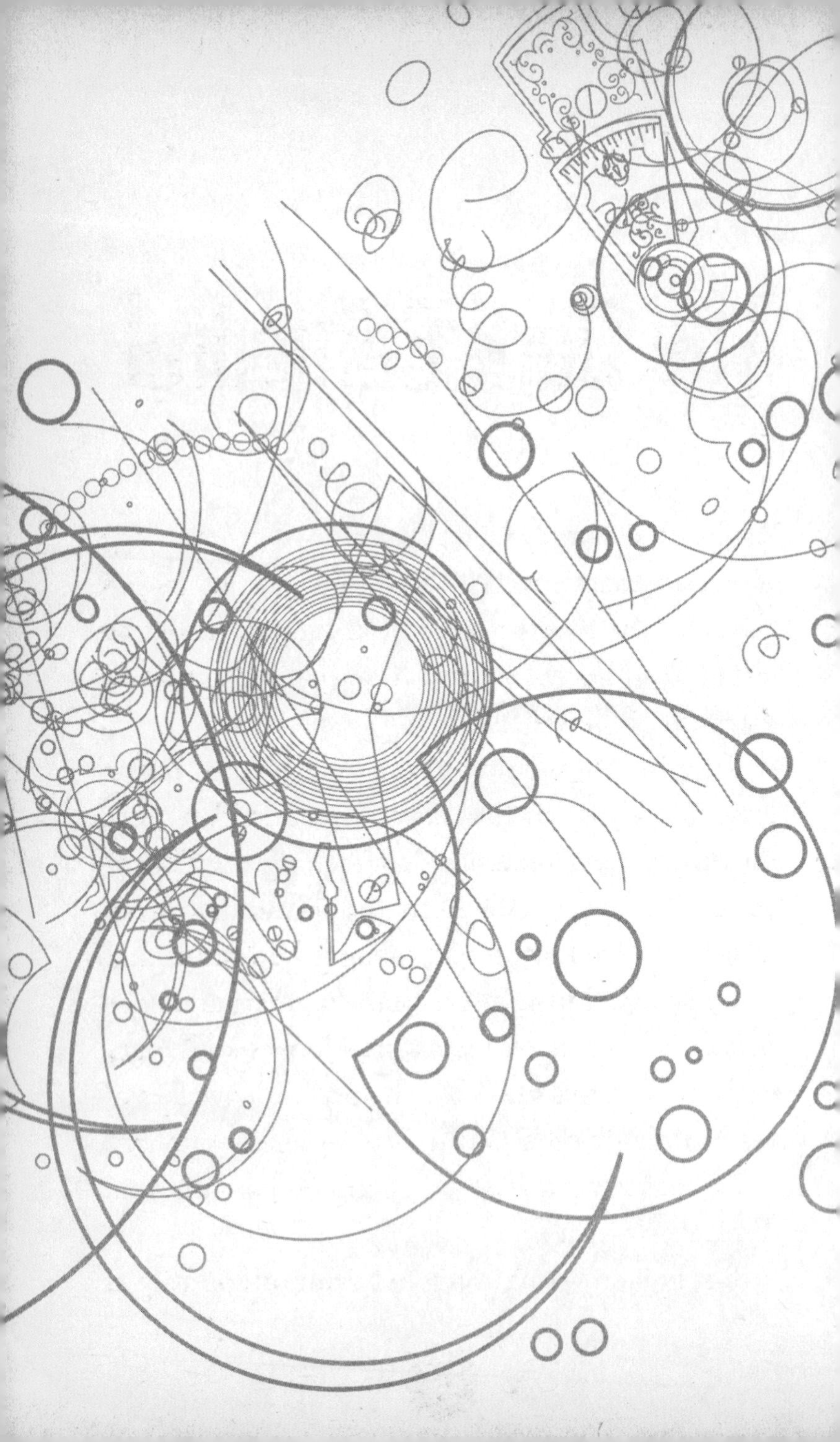

The Dark Cathedral

Lorton scrambled nimbly up to the next ridge of rock and peered cautiously over its jagged rim. The Doctor was still in sight, a little way ahead. And he still seemed to have no idea that he was being followed.

The climb was tiring in the intense heat, but at least it was easy to find cover now that they were on the craggy mountainside. Tracking the Doctor across the open plain from the village had been murder. Twice Lorton had thought he'd blown it.

Of course, I wouldn't have to sneak around at all if he'd just let me come along. He was still angry with the Doctor. Hadn't he helped him get free of his cell? Only to have the Doctor agree with Fra' Vallir that Lorton was 'too young' to go with him. Typical grown-up.

But Lorton wasn't going to be put off so easily. It

was *his* sister who was missing, after all. So he had shadowed the Doctor carefully as he paid a brief visit to the strange blue box that the scouting party had brought down from the cliff-top. Then, as the Doctor had set out alone, Lorton had followed.

A long, hot hike later, and here they were – nearing the summit of a craggy ridge that ran between two much higher peaks on either side. And Lorton still had no idea where they were headed.

The Doctor, who had been scaling a steep bank of dark rock just ahead, suddenly disappeared from view. *This must be it*, thought Lorton. *The summit.* He scrabbled quickly forward.

As he crested the ridge, the sight that met his eyes took his breath away. The Doctor was now standing only a few metres off, also transfixed. Lorton ducked down instinctively, then took in the amazing view.

Ahead of him, the land fell away steeply into a deep valley. From the mountainside that formed its opposite slope extended a vast, towering edifice of black stone. The massive building seemed to Lorton to radiate an overwhelming sense of malevolent power.

A horrific screech brought Lorton's mind abruptly back into focus. Something large and dark dropped suddenly out of the dazzling sky and plummeted towards the Doctor. As it dived, it emitted another ear-splitting scream.

Lorton saw the Doctor raise something with a bright blue tip, only to have it dashed from his hand by the swipe of a curved talon. As the Doctor stumbled and fell, the creature swooped low to slash at him. Then it rose once more, beating its large, leathery wings, preparing for another attack.

Lorton dug urgently in his pocket and withdrew his pouched sling-cord and a small white pebble – another float-stone, like the one he'd shown the Doctor. But this was one of half a dozen Lorton possessed that had been lovingly carved and smoothed, fine-tuned neither to rise nor fall, and to fly as true as a promise.

Lorton loaded the sling, took a deep breath, and stepped out from cover.

'Oi! Ugly!' he shouted.

The creature was hovering directly above the fallen Doctor, clearly preparing for a death-strike. But Lorton's yell drew its attention. It turned its thin red eyes towards him, sensing the chance of additional prey. With a series of powerful wing-beats, it sent itself swooping his way.

Just a little bit nearer, thought Lorton, whirling the slingshot rhythmically around his head, and trying to hold his nerve. *Must get a clear shot…*

As the flying creature bore down upon him, he unleashed the tiny white stone with all his skill and strength. It hurtled towards the attacking beast and caught it square in the throat. With a dreadful cry, the creature plummeted to the ground. It gave three agonised convulsions, then lay still.

Lorton let out a long sigh of relief. The Doctor quickly regained his feet, and came striding towards him, beaming broadly.

'Nice shot! Never seen a finer sling slung!'

The Doctor reached the spot where the dead creature lay. He stared at it, fascinated, then cautiously rolled it over with the toe of one shoe.

'What *is* this thing, anyway?'

'Rock spoorl,' replied Lorton. He approached, and knelt to retrieve his float-stone from beside the dead beast. 'Grandfather says they're quite common in the mountains. Those and cave scorpions. That's why I brought my sling.'

'Lucky for me you did, though unlucky for him.' The Doctor shook his head as if he actually felt sad for the vicious creature. Then he wrinkled his nose. 'Did your granddad tell you how revolting these things smell? Sort of rotten-egg-meets-Sontaran's-gym-socks. *Phew!*'

Lorton grinned. 'Wouldn't have bothered Grandfather. He's got no sense of smell. He did tell me what their weak spot is though – soft throat. The rest is tough as old boots.'

'Well, I'm sure he would have been impressed with the way you handled this one.' The Doctor ruffled Lorton's wild hair. Then his expression suddenly became stern. 'Though I think he'd be less chuffed that you've followed me out here against Fra' Vallir's orders…'

Lorton's grin faded.

'Buuut… what the heck!' continued the Doctor, brightening once more. 'You just saved my life – reckon that cancels out a bit of sneaking, don't you? Tell you what – if you watch my back, and promise to pick off any more flying stink-monsters, I'll let you tag along. Sound fair?'

Lorton beamed once more.

'Mind you,' said the Doctor, 'you might regret it.' He turned to look at the foreboding building looming across the valley. 'I reckon whoever calls that place Home Sweet Home is likely to be deadlier than a whole squadron of rock spoorls…'

They had descended about halfway down the treacherous valley side, moving silently in the shadow of the massive cathedral, when the Doctor suddenly gave a whoop of delight.

'You beauty! There she is!'

He scrabbled down the scree-covered incline and began hastily clearing an area of the rocky terrace at its base.

As Lorton joined him, he saw what the Doctor was excited about. An unnatural crack ran around a perfect square of rock. It was a door.

'Just where Vallir said it would be,' said the Doctor. 'The Dark Cathedral has exit tunnels running through this entire area. Only problem is how to get it open.'

Now that the Doctor had cleared the scree, Lorton could see that the stone hatchway was covered in an array of engraved symbols. A hairline crack ran around each one, as though marking individual stone buttons.

Lorton watched as the Doctor scanned the rock with his strange blue-tipped tool.

'The lock mechanism must be made of stone. Can't seem to pick up the right resonating frequency.'

He gestured to a single line of spidery engraving that ran below the rows of symbols.

'Does that mean anything to you?'

'It's Lithic script,' said Lorton. 'I'm not fluent, but I can make out some of it.' He pointed at one section of scrawl. 'This bit says "only the singular" or "the one alone" – something like that.'

The Doctor stared at the strange symbols silently for a few moments. Then his eyes lit up.

'Look! The symbols are in pairs! They're a bit higgledy-piggledy – some of them need turning round – but you can match each symbol up with another one the same!'

Lorton looked, and nodded. 'But there's an odd number of symbols,' the Doctor went on. 'So they can't *all* pair up. Maybe that's what the "singular" business is about – we have to find the odd one out!'

Activity

Which symbol is the odd one out?

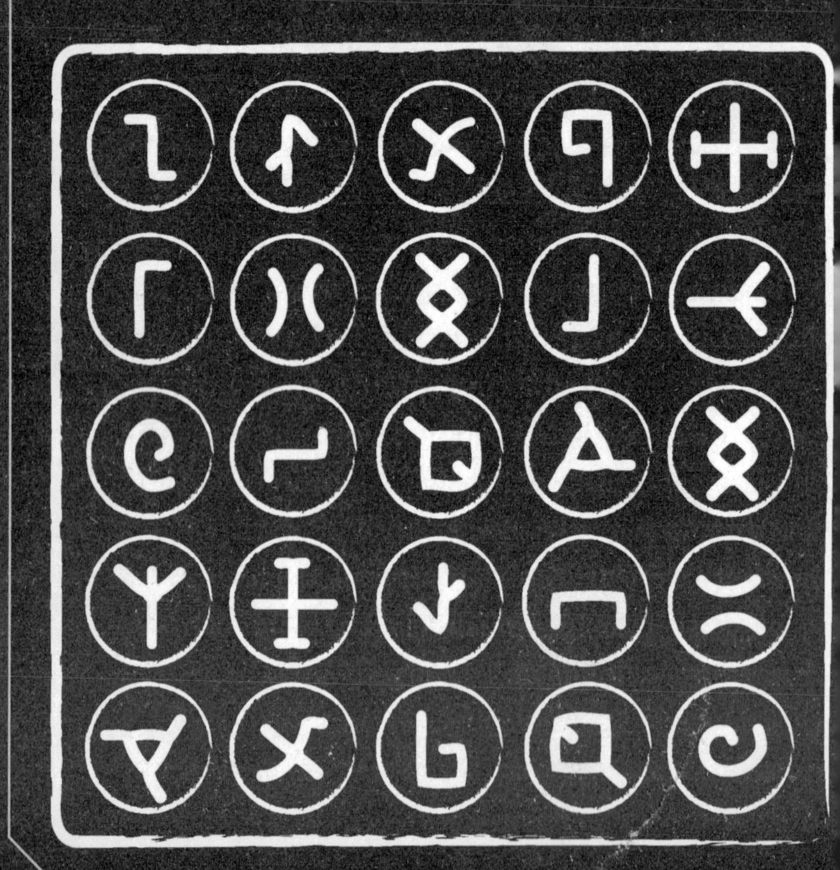

After a few minutes of concentration, they agreed on the symbol in the second last row, second from the right. The Doctor reached out to touch it. A moment later, its button sank into the surface of the stone. The entire square of rock dropped and slid smoothly aside, revealing the entrance to a narrow, darkened passageway below.

The Doctor grinned at Lorton. 'We're in!'

High Minister Drakon strode purposefully through the entrance to the Forge Chamber – and entered a world of heat, noise and industry. Half a dozen Brother technicians were carefully moving a huge crucible of molten metal to the far side of the chamber, where it was to be poured into giant casting moulds. Others were beating glowing blocks of hot steel into thin panels. And to one side of the entrance, a team of stone-techs were fitting a fresh batch of polished granite shields with their force-field circuitry.

Over the clang of hammer on anvil and the heavy thumps of component presses, Drakon barely heard Brother Ardos' yell of greeting. Ardos was standing beside a large stone plinth not far from the roaring mouth of the workshop's furnace.

He looked pleased. As Drakon joined him, he saw why. Stretched out on the plinth was a battered mechanical figure.

'The Agent! You have recovered it! And the Crystal itself?'

'Yes, High Minister, it was found with the Agent, at the site you specified. As we speak, my technicians are keying our scanning systems to the Crystal's molecular structure, so that we can track its location more accurately in future. It will be brought to you directly.'

'Good work, Brother. And what of the Agent itself? What news does it bring of the traitor Varlos?'

Ardos looked sombre. 'As you can see, the Agent suffered extensive damage in the crash-landing. Its systems are in emergency hibernation. We have yet to retrieve any information from its data core. As soon as Sister Clathine and I have made the necessary repairs to reactivate it, it will deliver a full report to the Witan.'

'High Minister Drakon!'

Drakon turned to find Sister Hellan behind him.

'Apologies for the interruption, High Minister,' continued Hellan, 'but you have a visitor.'

The translucent-yellow skin of Drakon's forehead wrinkled in a frown.

'A visitor?'

'Yes, High Minister. A "John Smith". Special Envoy of the Spiel Confederation. He claims to have a business proposal. I've had him held under guard.'

Drakon exchanged puzzled looks with Ardos, then turned to leave.

'Very well. We will grant this John Smith an audience. Though he is most unwise to enter the Dark Cathedral uninvited…'

Strange Meetings

It's easy to see why they call it the Dark Cathedral, thought Lorton.

The entrance tunnel had been dingy enough, but here inside the heart of the Cathedral it was almost pitch black. The blue glow of the Doctor's silver gadget had helped illuminate things for a while. But now that the Doctor had left him, Lorton had to cope with the inky darkness around him as best he could.

I thought I'd had enough sunshine to last a lifetime. But right now, I'd give anything for a bit of daylight.

He inched his way along the passage, running his left hand along the cold stone wall as a guide, and marvelling that the Darksmiths could survive in these murky conditions. He could barely see a metre ahead. How was he ever going to find Beth?

That was the plan. To try and find his sister and the other children, while the Doctor took care of some 'private business' he had with the Darksmiths.

'I'll be back in no time!' The Doctor had reassured him. 'Well, not exactly *no* time. That would be a TARDIS job. But as soon as I can, I'll come back and find you. Then we'll see what we can do about getting your sister and her friends out of here!'

But what if we're already too late? Lorton hoped desperately that Bethin was still OK. She could be a bit bossy sometimes, sure. But since their parents died, she had done her best to look out for him. He wasn't going to let her down now.

His guiding hand suddenly slipped into thin air. There was an opening in the left wall. He moved awkwardly to the other wall and found that it, too, ceased abruptly. But moving cautiously forward led him straight into cold stone. He was at a T-junction.

As he stood in the darkness, wondering which route to follow, Lorton's nose picked up a faint but familiar smell. Orange blossom. The scent seemed to be coming from along the passage on the right. And Lorton could remember the last time he had smelt it – when the Dreamspinner had come to his village.

Without further hesitation, he began making his way blindly along the right-hand passageway.

A blue light flared into life in the darkness. As the Doctor held his sonic screwdriver high, it cast an eerie glow over his surroundings.

He was standing in a cavernous underground chamber. Its vaulted ceiling was supported by thick granite pillars. Each was intricately carved, as was the arched ceiling itself.

'Wow. Impressive. Someone around here is *seriously* handy with a stone chisel.'

A massive stone table stood at the centre of the chamber. Around it were seated nine figures, in hooded cloaks. All were shielding their eyes against the sonic's blue glow, clearly dazzled.

'Ah – sorry about that folks!' The Doctor grinned broadly. 'But it's blacker than a black hole in a power cut down here. Thought I'd shed a little light on the situation.'

The grey-cloaked figure at the centre of the table threw back his hood to reveal a skeletal face, thinly covered by translucent, gel-like flesh. He scowled at the Doctor, then spoke in a low, rasping voice.

'The Darksmiths of Karagula have no need of light! We despise it! From darkness comes power, creation and truth!'

'If you say so,' replied the Doctor pleasantly.

'I am Drakon, High Minister of the Witan, voice of the Darksmith Collective,' continued the figure in grey. 'State your business with this council, John Smith.'

'Right. Yes.' The Doctor looked sombre. 'Well, as I told the gentleman earlier, I'm here on behalf of the Spiel Confederation. We govern a system of planets in the Blarney Cluster. It's a system that's always enjoyed great prosperity. Until recently.'

'Explain,' Drakon commanded.

'Well, our wealth is due almost entirely to the Blarnian Twaddle, a native species of my home-world. Its eggs are highly valued for their healing powers, and fetch a good price. But about ten years ago, the Twaddle began to die out – nobody knows why. Then one day, no more Twaddle. And now the species has been declared extinct.'

'What is this to do with us?' another of the cloaked figures rasped.

'Well, because we want to rebuild the Twaddle population and the trade it supports. Which means bringing at least one breeding pair back to life.'

The Doctor gestured to the council members with his sonic, causing them to flinch back from its light. 'That's where you lot come in. Amongst other things, you have a reputation for being able to create life from inanimate matter, I'm told.'

Several of the Witan exchanged shifty glances.

'So!' The Doctor looked round the shadowed faces eagerly. 'A device that could bring dead remains back to life – does that sound like something you might be able to rustle up for us? Money no object, of course…'

High Minister Drakon signalled for the muttering around him to cease. He shook his skull-like head slowly. 'Such a commission is beyond our powers. Not even we can bring the dead to life.'

'Funny,' said the Doctor, 'because the word on the intergalactic grapevine is that one of you – a Mister Varlos, is it? – has already created –'

Drakon cut in, his tone menacing.

'*Former* Brother Varlos is no longer one of the Collective. The commission you refer to was a unique contract, undertaken for a unique client. It was unsuccessful.'

The Doctor held Drakon's cold gaze for a

moment, then shrugged.

'Fair enough. Disappointing, but can't be helped. You wouldn't lie, I'm sure. Let's face it – ' the Doctor grinned, '– I'd see right through you! Still,' he continued, 'while I'm here, perhaps I could take a look at the sort of stuff you *do* take on? In case there's anything the Confederation might be interested in.'

Drakon paused, then nodded. He turned to address one of his hooded colleagues.

'Brother Jaxal. Escort our visitor to the Cathedral Library.' He looked back at the Doctor. 'Our trading registers contain details of all the contracts we have undertaken since the Collective was founded, together with testimonials from satisfied clients and favourable reviews from the major lifestyle magazines where appropriate. And where the contracts are not strictly confidential, of course, you may browse them at will.'

'Brilliant. Thanks!'

Drakon rose to his feet, signalling that the interview was over. Brother Jaxal hurriedly led the Doctor to the chamber's main doors. As they closed behind them, Drakon turned to the crimson-cloaked minister at his side.

'Brother Talen – check the stranger's story on our systems immediately. There is more to this John Smith than meets the eye, I fear…'

Lorton silently descended the last few steps of the spiralling stone staircase. The scent of orange blossom had grown ever stronger as he had followed its trail, first along the darkened passageway and now down these winding steps.

Fortunately, the darkness had gradually receded a little. He had been able to make his way much more easily by the pale green light that faintly illuminated the passage, coming from somewhere up ahead.

Now, as he stepped through the doorway at the foot of the staircase into the chamber beyond, Lorton could see the light's source. In one corner of the square stone room stood an upright silver box. Its entire upper half pulsed with green light. It was connected by cables to a number of smaller devices scattered on the floor around it.

But it was what lay in the other corner that immediately became the focus of Lorton's attention. A creature unlike anything he had ever seen before. Its grotesque body looked like some bizarre biological mix-and-match experiment, with insect-like limbs grafted to a reptilian body, and those huge, horribly damaged eyes...

'I smell your fear, child.'

The creature's speech was accompanied by moist clicking sounds as its bizarre mouthparts moved across one another. It stalked a little way towards Lorton, then paused. He saw a series of narrow, gill-like slits open in both sides of the creature's neck, and heard the hiss of air being drawn into them.

'And yet there is a whiff of courage about you, too – the same stench as on that stubborn girl-child.' The creature inhaled again. 'Yes, you share the same olfactory profile. She is your sister, perhaps?'

It meant Bethin, Lorton knew. Somehow this... *thing* was involved in her abduction. His fear gave way to a surge of anger.

'What have you done with her!'

The creature's mouthparts clicked rhythmically, almost as though it was tut-tut-tutting. 'Such anger! You reek of aggression, boy.' It moved a little closer. 'Perhaps you would be calmer if I were to assume a more... familiar appearance?'

Lorton heard a faint hissing sound. His image of the creature suddenly began to blur, as though slipping out of focus. A moment later, it had vanished completely. In its place stood an attractive woman in pale blue robes, smiling sweetly at him.

A toolkit stood open among the devices on the chamber floor. Lorton bent to snatch up a metal bar from it, then faced the woman, wielding it threateningly.

'I asked you what you've done with my sister!'

The woman's eyes narrowed in cruel disdain, and her smile became mocking. 'Your weapon is pointless child. I will not attack you physically. There is no need, when I can so easily paralyse your mind…'

There was another faint hiss. To his horror, Lorton saw a dozen sinuous black shapes begin oozing from the stone walls of the chamber around him. They slipped to the floor, snakelike, and started slithering towards him. They were eyeless, but had wide mouths, lined with multiple sets of razor-sharp teeth.

Lorton was seized by utter terror. The bar slipped uselessly from his grasp. The monsters slithering towards him were the stuff of his darkest dreams. He reacted instinctively, in the way any child confronted by their worst nightmare would.

He threw back his head and screamed and screamed.

In The Library

Brother Jaxal heaved the next volume of the trade register from his library trolley onto the stone desk. He had his eyes screwed up, as though the light by which the Doctor was reading – the pale glow of his sonic screwdriver – caused him pain. He retreated silently to the dark aisles of stone-built shelving to continue his search for further documents.

The Doctor dragged the massive tome across in front of him. Like the previous volumes, its jacket was made of thick slate, or something like it. He lifted the heavy front cover, and touched the dark, smooth slab within. Its blank surface instantly transformed, becoming pitted with line upon line of engraved text. The Doctor read this first page, then tapped the slab again. The original engravings faded as a whole new page of inscribed text appeared.

The registers made impressive reading. At one time or another, the Darksmiths had crafted more or less every variety of technological device, from matter-transfer systems to supra-lightspeed engines. Even the famous Mortal Mirror that the Doctor had himself encountered... Their trademark seemed to be the use of both ancient and highly advanced technologies, often combined in a single project. They had fulfilled contracts for many wealthy and powerful clients, from many galaxies.

But like the previous volumes the Doctor had searched, this one contained no mention of Varlos, or the Eternity Crystal. His quest to find out more about the strange Crystal – to understand why it had been created, and how it had brought about the bizarre events on Earth's Moon and the cemetery world of Mordane – seemed in vain.

Jaxal approached again, with another hefty volume on his trolley. As the Doctor looked up at him, he saw the librarian glance anxiously at a small stone door in the nearby wall. The third time the Doctor had caught him doing so.

The Doctor closed the book and heaved it aside. 'Talk about heavy reading!' He looked back to Jaxal. 'By the way, I meant to ask – since this is a library, can I take something out?'

The librarian looked at him warily. 'What?'

'Well – *you*, actually...'

Before Jaxal could react, the Doctor raised the tip of his sonic to the librarian's temple. Jaxal slumped to the floor, unconscious. The Doctor checked Jaxal's life-signs, then crossed quickly to the door that the librarian had been eyeing nervously.

'Now – let's see what you were so keen I shouldn't see...'

But the door was locked. And like the one that he and Lorton had encountered earlier, it was unaffected by his sonic screwdriver.

'Maybe if I adjust the resonating frequency manually...' muttered the Doctor, fiddling with the sonic screwdriver's settings. He scanned it slowly around the door's edge again. This time, there was the satisfying *clunk* of a heavy lock releasing. As the Doctor leaned on the door, it swung slowly open.

The Doctor found himself in a small, bare room, occupied by only a stone table and chair. A large book, similar to the volumes he had already looked through, lay on the table. He crossed to take a closer look.

The book's cover was entirely blank apart from

the faint impression of a stylised black flame – the symbol of the Darksmiths. When the Doctor tried to open it, he couldn't.

Then he noticed a second, much smaller book – a notepad, perhaps – lying on the table with a slim black stylus beside it. This one opened easily. As it did so, several lines of hand-written text immediately appeared on the slab inside:

Date: 42 / 13 / 34 / 78
Access to Varlos's journal still denied.
No progress in overriding locking system.

The Doctor felt a tingle of excitement. So the larger book was actually Brother Varlos' journal. This was more like it.

Keeping its settings the same, he gingerly ran the sonic screwdriver around the edges of the large stone book. Nothing happened.

It took him several minutes experimenting with different settings before anything did happen. Then, suddenly, there was a rough, grating noise, and the front cover of the book transformed before the Doctor's eyes. A hidden panel slid open in the lower part, revealing a row of five barrel-like stone dials.

Activity

What are the five numbers hidden in the text?

THESTONEMANINEACH

OFOURSOULSEVEN

DEATHCANNOTWOUND

Enter your Answers:

ONE, NINE
FOUR, SEVEN
TWO

Above the panel, parts of the cover's stone surface sank away, creating several lines of inscription:

The stone man in each
of our souls even
death cannot wound

The Doctor hastily examined the dials. There was a digit engraved on each. 'Standard combination lock,' he muttered to himself, 'only made of stone.'

He stared at the text, puzzled. Was it a Darksmith proverb? A riddle perhaps? Somehow, it concealed the combination for the numerical lock, he was certain. He grabbed the notebook and stylus and copied down the cryptic text, one letter immediately after the next, to see if this revealed anything.

Moments later, the Doctor gave a whoop of triumph. He hurriedly set the numbered dials to the five-digit combination he had uncovered. First one, then nine, followed by four then seven and finally two.

With a rasping sound, the entire front cover of the book slid aside, into its spine. The dark slab that was revealed beneath it carried another inscription:

The Eternity Device:
A development journal
by Astrule Varlos

'Gotcha!' murmured the Doctor. He tapped the slab again, then again. Page after page of text and diagrams appeared in turn.

The Doctor heaved the book onto its right-hand edge and examined its thick spine. Yes, there it was. A small, circular socket set in the stone. A data-transfer port. It must have revealed itself when he cracked the combination.

He quickly inserted the unlit end of his sonic screwdriver into the data-port. There was a series of whirrs and clicks as it adapted itself to the socket's configuration. Then its blue tip began to flicker and pulse.

A few seconds ought to do it, thought the Doctor. That was all it should take for the entire contents of Varlos' journal to be uploaded to the TARDIS data banks. He could look through it in detail once he had recovered the Crystal.

Less than a minute later, the Doctor was back in the main library, heading for the exit. Jaxal would be coming round soon, so he had to make himself scarce. The Doctor slipped out into the dark passageway, once more using the sonic to light his way.

Now, if I were a Darksmith, where would I keep –

The Doctor's thoughts were cut short by a blood-chilling sound. The sound of a young boy's terrified screams…

The Colour of Darkness

The Doctor tore down the spiralling stone staircase. He was breathless now, having run at full pelt along one dark passageway after another. As he reached the bottom step, another nerve-jarring scream split the air from just beyond the doorway ahead.

He rummaged urgently through his jacket pockets, pulled out an ordinary household clothes peg, and clamped it over his nose. Then he strode purposefully through the doorway into the chamber beyond.

Lorton was writhing on the stone floor of the chamber, ashen-faced and wide-eyed with fear, his arms thrashing wildly. It was as though he was trying to fend off some terrifying, invisible assailant.

At the other side of the chamber crouched a

large creature. It was calmly watching the young boy's frenzied struggle. *Only it can't be watching*, thought the Doctor. Its huge eyes were horridly damaged, clearly blind.

The Doctor hurried to Lorton's aid. 'Hold your nose!' he yelled. 'Whatever you think you're seeing, it's not real! Hold your nose!'

His peculiar advice must have reached some part of the boy's tortured mind. Lorton pinched his nose between finger and thumb. Almost at once, his struggling began to subside.

The Doctor helped the boy, still trembling uncontrollably, into a sitting position. Then he turned to confront the creature angrily.

'This your idea of fun, is it? Scaring the living daylights out of a child?'

The creature didn't respond. Instead, it inhaled deeply, it neck-slits gaping to let air hiss wetly past. Then it spoke. 'Your scent is rather…' – its mouthparts *click-clicked* as though seeking the correct word – '…*unusual*.'

'Oh, that's nice!' said the Doctor. 'If we're getting personal, that flowery stuff you reek of smells pretty cheap.'

The creature reared up. 'Every odour I emit has

been expertly crafted!' it spat. 'Every vapour has a calculated effect, a unique purpose!'

The Doctor looked unimpressed. "That's your thing, isn't it? Smells. That's how you brainwash people. Who exactly *are* you?'

'I am Shas-Raklat.' The creature's name sounded like the rattle of bones. 'I am one of the Menim.' The Doctor frowned. 'But I thought the Menim were renowned for their *visual* sense...'

'Your knowledge serves you well. Since the depths of time, my race has been famed for its power of sight. Menim eyes can see in higher definition, recognise greater subtleties of colour and form, than those of any other race.'

'But not yours, eh?' The Doctor's tone became sympathetic. 'What happened to them?'

The creature paused. 'My eyes were put out by my own kind,' it said, darkly, 'as a punishment.'

'Blimey. What did you do?'

The creature's temper flared again. 'It is of no matter! But can you imagine what it was like to have inhabited a world of infinite colours, then to be cast into one where there were none? Only the colour of darkness...'

'It must have been terrible,' replied the

Doctor sincerely.

'It drove me to the brink of madness! But I survived. I resolved to find a new way of seeing. Through olfaction – through my sense of smell.'

The creature turned its head first one way, then the other. Clusters of electronic components, together with patches of something flesh-like, were grafted to either side of its neck. Wires running from them punctured the creature's skin.

'For many years I have worked on enhancing my olfactory system. My modifications have magnified my sense of smell many thousands of times. I now see the world as clearly as before. But my colours are aromas, my light and shade different nuances of scent.'

'And I bet you synthesise your own odours too, don't you?' said the Doctor.

'My abilities have given me unprecedented knowledge of how different odours work upon the mind. I have learned to mix vapours that have whatever effect I desire on those who inhale them. I can alter memories, create visions, stimulate pleasurable emotions. There are many who will pay handsomely for such fantasies.'

'So you're a drug dealer, basically.'

'I am an artist!' clacked the enraged creature. 'A genius of olfactory illusion –'

'Yeah, yeah,' interrupted the Doctor. 'But this smelly-mind-control rubbish of yours isn't exactly super-effective, is it? I mean, look at me and my young friend here. All we have to do is block our noses!'

The creature hissed menacingly.

'Then perhaps I shall have to resort to more... *basic* methods.'

It lifted its scaly tail high over its back. With a sickening squelch, a long spike slid out from its bulbous end. Yellow liquid oozed from the tail-spike's tip. The creature began to advance.

'Ah, well...' The Doctor did his best to seem unfazed. 'When you put it like that...'

He turned to help Lorton unhurriedly to his feet, smiling reassuringly. Then his expression suddenly changed to one of wide-eyed urgency.

'Run!!'

TARDIS Data-Bank

Olfaction

Olfaction is the sense of smell. It relies on special sensory cells that can detect small traces of chemicals, called odours, in the medium in which an organism is living.

RECEPTOR CELLS

Olfactory receptor cells are found in different locations in different species: in the nose-lining of humans and other terrestrial vertebrates; on the antennae of insects; above the central mouth of Myxilinic frost-worms from the planet Myxilinis Minima.

SENSITIVITY

Some species have a more powerful olfactory system than others. A bloodhound's sense of smell is several million times more sensitive than a human's. Salmon smell their way back to their birthplace, often swimming thousands of miles to get there.

PHEROMONES

Special odours, called pheromones, are used by many organisms for communication. For instance, the alpha-female in each Mantis colony on Parap IV – like the terrestrial Honeybee queen – releases pheromones that control the activity of her entire hive.

SMELL AND MEMORY

In humans, smell is the most closely linked sense to memory. This is because olfaction uses the same part of the brain – called the limbic system – that handles memories and emotion.

It was only after they had put the spiral staircase and several corridors between them and the alien creature that the Doctor and Lorton came to a stop.

Lorton was the first to speak, between panting breaths. 'So that thing… uses smells… to mess with people's minds?'

The Doctor, bent forward, hands on his thighs as he caught his breath, nodded.

'Is that how it made everyone believe that their dreams had come true?' Lorton asked. 'How it made me imagine those horrible snake things?'

'You've got it,' confirmed the Doctor. 'Aroma-hypnosis. Smell control.' He reached for the peg on his nose. 'Right – think I can safely remove my olfactory blocker.'

He unclipped the peg and gave his nose a good rub. 'Ooh – that's better. Not very comfy, a clothes peg on the nose. And hopeless for running.'

'But how did you know?' quizzed Lorton.

'Your grandfather,' replied the Doctor. 'He saw our friend back there for what she was right from the beginning, didn't he? The vapour she used to make everyone else perceive her in humanoid form – the pretty lady in the blue dress – didn't work on him. Why not? You told me yourself – *he has no sense of smell*. I should have figured it out sooner.'

'But why did she go to all that trouble at the village just to get hold of the children? What does she want them for?'

The Doctor's expression darkened. 'I'm afraid that's the really creepy bit. Some of those "modifications" to Shas-Raklat's olfactory system were transplanted biological tissue. And the sensory organs of the young are always more receptive.' He grimaced, and went on: 'I'm afraid she wants your sister and the others for olfactory spare parts. Nose transplants. Not nice.'

Lorton went rather pale.

'My guess is that she's struck a deal with the Darksmiths,' continued the Doctor. 'In exchange for her providing a few batches of sweet-dreams-in-a-bottle for them to sniff up and enjoy, they've agreed to turn a blind eye to her abducting a few locals.'

'We've got to stop her!'

'And quickly,' agreed the Doctor. 'That glowing thing in her chamber back there was charging a set of light-drive cells. Which means she's planning to leave Karagula soon.'

Lorton looked horrified.

'But,' continued the Doctor, more brightly, 'it

also means she's got a spacecraft parked somewhere. If we can find out where *that* is, then we'll find your sister.' He gave Lorton an encouraging wink. 'And I know just where to look…'

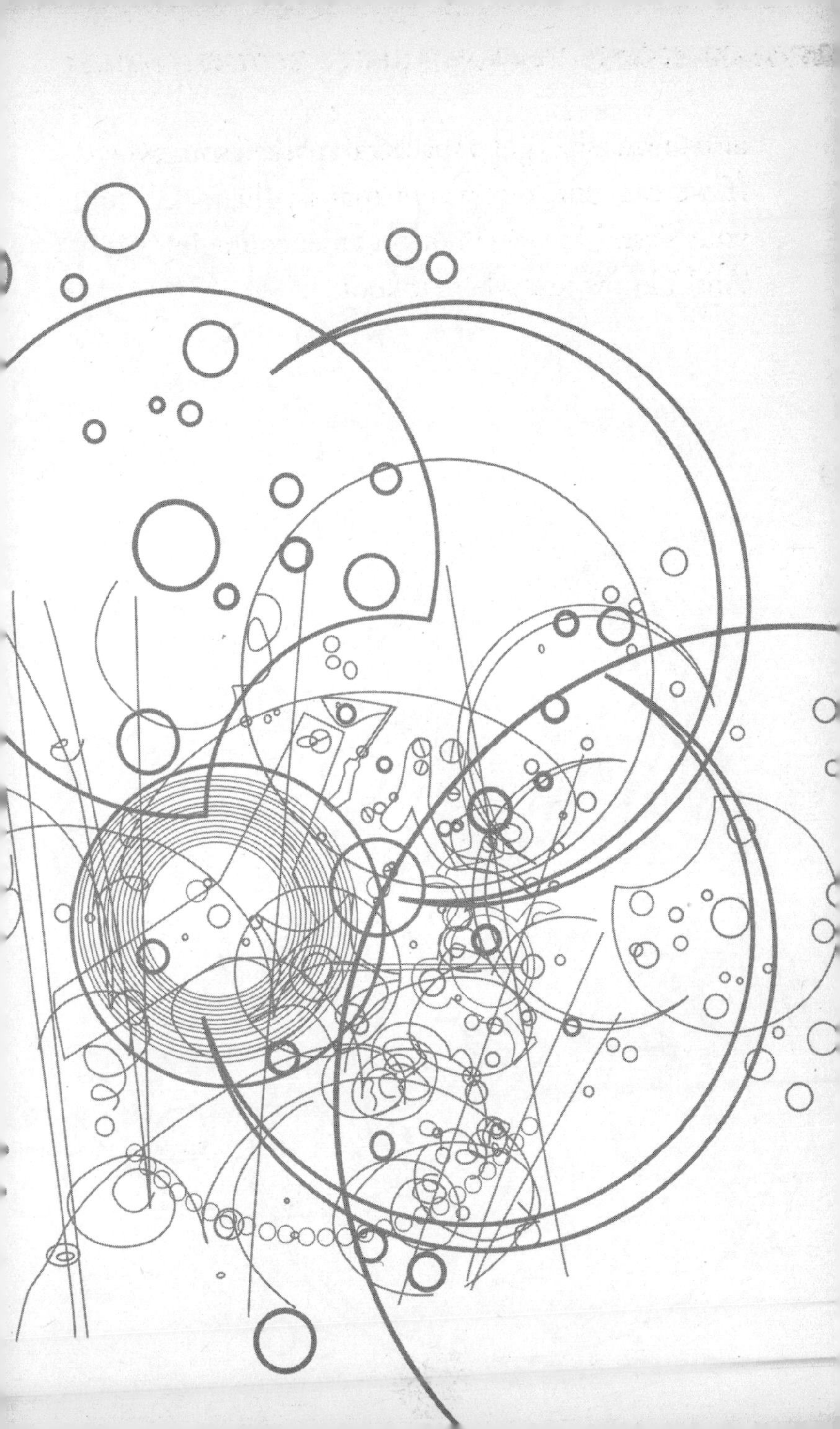

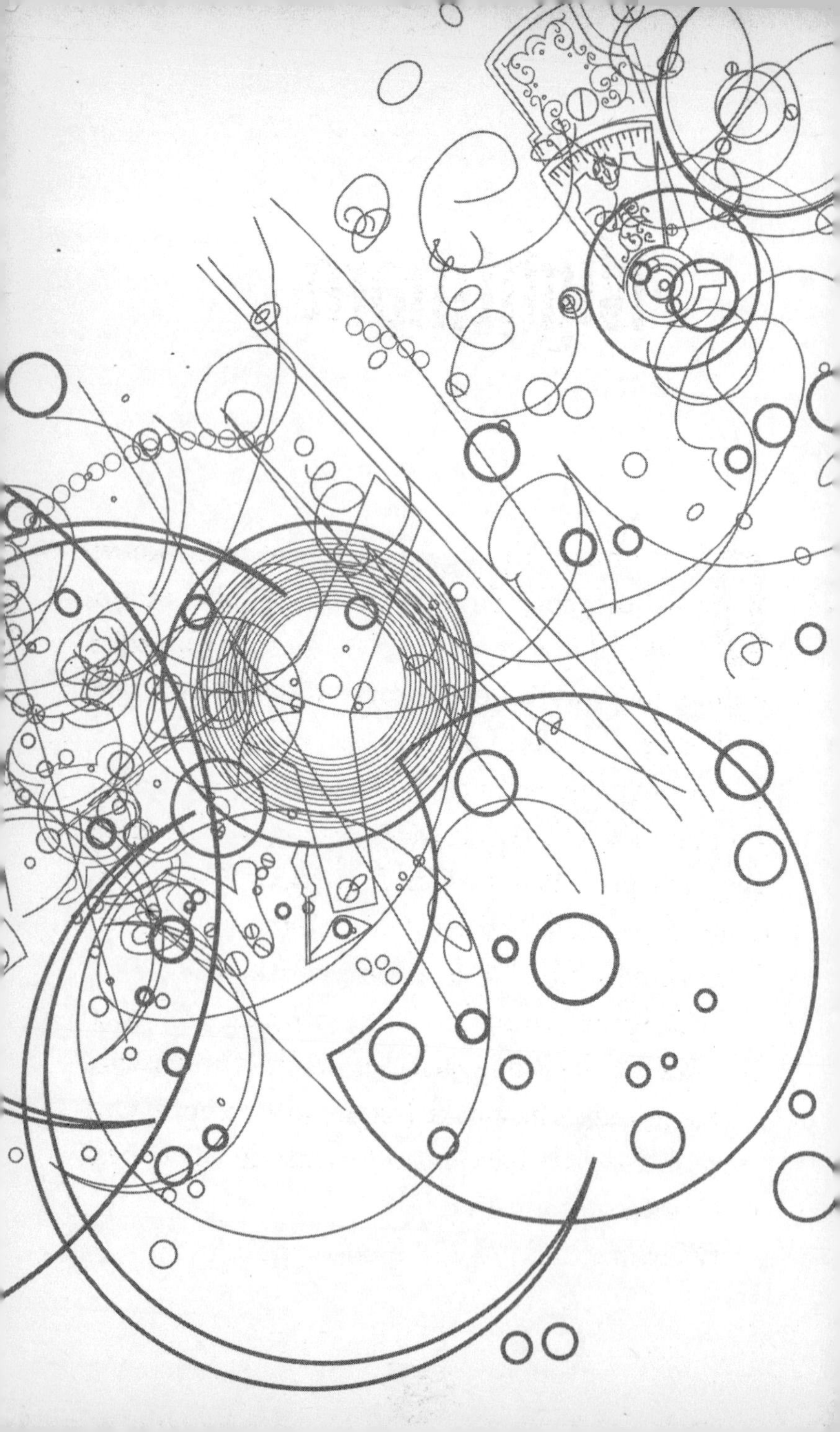

Nightmare

One moment, the Agent's artificial mind knew only the cold white stillness of hibernation mode. The next, as its core systems came back online, its powerful processors suddenly streamed with silver threads of data.

Within nanoseconds, the robot's reactivated programs had retrieved the error log that detailed the damage it had sustained in its crash-landing. One by one, its systems ran diagnostic checks. Everything seemed to have been repaired.

The Agent swung its heavy metallic legs over the side of the stone slab on which it was lying, and stood up. The cloaked figure of Brother Ardos stood beside the slab, eagerly watching the revival of his awesome creation.

'Welcome back, Agent. Status report!'

'All systems fully functional,' boomed the robot.

Ardos looked smug – then somewhat surprised as the robot continued.

'Scanners detect two unauthorised life forms in Area Twelve. Infra-red body-heat profiles indicate one intruder has alien cardiac morphology. Profile matches to known enemy.'

'What?' Ardos was thoroughly confused. 'What do you mean? Clarify report!'

'The Doctor,' thundered the Agent. 'The Doctor is in the Cathedral. He is heading for the hangar. This unit advises that he should be stopped.'

'Voilà! The hangar!'

The Doctor grinned at Lorton's dumbfounded look as the boy took in the massive underground chamber, and the large matt-black craft squatting at its centre.

'And that little beauty must be our alien friend's personal runabout.'

It was hard to make out much detail of Shas-Raklat's ship. The only illumination in the hangar – other than the pale blue glow of the Doctor's sonic screwdriver – came from an open hatchway in the spacecraft's near side. But even in the gloom, the teardrop-shaped ship looked sleek and powerful.

'Come on.' The Doctor strode eagerly across the hangar. 'Let's have a look inside.'

The door of the spacecraft's open hatchway formed an access ramp. It led them into the ship's main control area. Banks of consoles surrounded a large, oddly-shaped chair, presumably designed to fit Shas-Raklat's bizarre body.

'I'm going to look for Beth,' said Lorton, and disappeared along a corridor that led further into the heart of the spaceship.

The Doctor was admiring a collection of thousands of transparent phials held in row upon row of racking against one wall of the control cabin. Some appeared empty. Inside others he could make out pale clouds of faintly coloured vapour.

'The Dreamspinner's store cupboard,' he muttered to himself. 'Each one an instant vision, a bottled dream...'

He picked up a phial clouded with dark grey vapour and swirled it in front of his eyes. '...or a nightmare –'

'Doctor! I've found her!'

At Lorton's urgent yell, the Doctor slipped the vapour phial into his jacket pocket and hurried after him.

The passageway led to a narrow hold. Against its side walls were pinned the bodies of over fifty children, held in place by cocoons of clinging green film. Lorton had found his sister at the far end of the hold.

'Is she dead?' he asked.

The Doctor hastily scanned the tip of his sonic across the girl's forehead. 'No. She's in some sort of trance.'

Thin transparent tubes protruded from both the girl's nostrils. The Doctor wrenched them free. A moment later, Bethin's head swayed to one side, and they saw her body stir under the green film.

Together they tore the cocoon away, and lowered the dazed girl gently onto the floor. Her eyes opened, and she gave Lorton a weak smile. Her brother beamed back, and hugged her warmly.

The Doctor waited a few minutes while Bethin came round. Then he took Lorton aside. 'Now listen. I want you and your sister to revive all the other children as quickly as you can. You've seen what to do. Then lead them out of this place the way we came in. Get yourselves back to your village. Can you do that?'

Lorton nodded decisively.

The Doctor grinned. 'Good man!'

As Lorton immediately began removing the nasal tubes from the other children, the Doctor turned and made his way back to the spacecraft's access hatch. It was time he got back to fulfilling his main purpose – the quest that had brought him to Karagula. Time to find the Crystal. He hurried down the access ramp into the gloom of the hangar.

'But what about you, Doctor?' Lorton called after him. 'Why aren't you coming with us?'

The Doctor strode back to Lorton and laid a hand on his shoulder. 'Don't worry – I'll make my own way out soon enough. I just need to find something that the Darksmiths took from me –'

'I think you mean that we took *back* from you, Doctor.'

The Doctor spun round in alarm at the sound of High Minister Drakon's sinister voice. The Darksmith leader was standing in the hangar entrance. He was accompanied by another cloaked figure, half a dozen guards in gleaming battle armour, and the towering mechanical hulk of the Agent.

'It is "Doctor", isn't it?' rasped Drakon sarcastically.

'Not "John Smith" after all? May I introduce my fellow minister, Brother Ardos. I believe you've already met his magnificent robotic creation. It has been telling us all about your interest in our property.'

His thin, translucent arm emerged from beneath his grey cloak. His skeletal hand held a large, egg-shaped Crystal that glowed with a faint blue light.

'The Eternity Crystal. This is what you seek, is it not?' Drakon stared silently at the jewel for a moment. Then his lidless eyes narrowed as he snarled at the Doctor. 'You will die before you possess it again!'

'I don't want to possess it!' insisted the Doctor. 'I just want to keep it out of harm's way. I don't think you've got the slightest idea just how dangerous that thing is.'

'You insult our intelligence!' screeched Drakon. 'It was a Darksmith who created the Crystal, who crafted it from raw matter with skills only our race command!'

'Maybe,' conceded the Doctor. 'But even Varlos had second thoughts about handing it over to whoever ordered it, didn't he? Otherwise why did he hide it on the Moon?'

'Enough!' Drakon raised his free hand, and the six armour-clad guards strode forward and unsheathed their weapons – two-handed swords that fizzed with blue energy. The Agent, too, stepped heavily forward.

The High Minister gave a cruel sneer. 'Either surrender, Doctor, or meet your death!'

The Doctor looked undecided for a few moments, then gave a defeated sigh. 'OK. Not much of a choice is it?' He gestured to Lorton, still beside him. 'Just give me a second to convince my young friend here to come quietly. He's a bit feisty. Doesn't generally do surrender.'

The Doctor turned and leaned close to Lorton, as though speaking coaxingly to him. 'You still got that slingshot?' he whispered, with a meaningful look.

Lorton, hidden from the Darksmiths' view by the Doctor's body, slipped the sling discreetly from his pocket.

'Well done!' hissed the Doctor. 'I need you to take out the big metal guy. Aim for the panel on his left side. Looks like the controls for his auxiliary systems. Might slow him down for a bit.'

It was the Doctor's turn to slip something secretively from his jacket pocket – the small phial of dark vapour. 'This ought to sort the rest of them. Best hold your breath…' He gave Lorton a wild grin, eyes sparkling. 'This'll be something to tell your granddad. Ready?'

Lorton took in a long breath, then nodded.

'OK… Now!'

The Doctor spun suddenly. With his best baseball pitch, he hurled the phial at the stone floor just in front of the Darksmith group.

The phial smashed, releasing a thin wisp of grey vapour, which quickly dispersed. Almost immediately, shrieks of raw terror came from the Darksmiths. The armed guards dropped their weapons and ran.

The Doctor's gamble was working – whatever olfactory illusion Shas-Raklat had bottled in the phial was scaring the living daylights out of Drakon's cronies.

But not Drakon.

'It's a trick, you weak-minded fools! An illusion!' raged the High Minister, his bony hand clasped to his nose. 'Come back!'

The Agent, too, stood its ground.

'Kill them!' Drakon screamed at the robot, thrusting a translucent finger at the Doctor.

But Lorton was ready. As the Doctor had thrown the phial and stepped aside, Lorton had immediately begun whirling his slingshot. Now he unleashed its float-stone missile.

The small white stone flew true as an arrow, striking the Agent's auxiliary control panel. The impact triggered the massive robot's rocket thrusters. They flared into life, sending the Agent rocketing upwards and sideways, out of control.

Drakon was sent sprawling by the Agent's unplanned take-off. As he hit the floor, the Eternity Crystal spilled from his bony grasp.

The Doctor seized his chance. Darting forward, he snatched the rolling Crystal from the floor, then turned for the spaceship.

'Get on board!' he yelled at Lorton, sprinting for the access ramp.

A moment later, his path was blocked by the powerful figure of the Agent, as it landed heavily just ahead of him. The Doctor froze, helpless, as the robot levelled its arm-mounted lasers at him.

But the blasts that shook the hangar an instant later didn't come from the Agent's weapons. Instead, they came from a gun turret mounted on top of Shas-Raklat's spaceship. The wild barrage of laser fire hit the stone floor just beside the Agent, sending it lurching to one side.

The Doctor looked up to see Bethin, eyes wild and teeth gritted, wrestling with the controls inside the turret's transparent bubble.

'Nice one!'

The Doctor gave the young girl an enthusiastic thumbs-up. Before the Agent could regain its footing, he sprinted past it and raced up the access ramp. Lorton hurriedly hit the switch to seal the hatch behind him.

There was a dull thud and the Doctor and Lorton both staggered as the ship shook violently. The Agent was directing its firepower at the spacecraft's exterior.

'What now?' asked Lorton desperately. 'We're trapped!'

The Doctor pocketed the Crystal, then dashed to the ship's flight controls, where he began frantically tapping buttons and throwing switches.

'Bethin!' he yelled. The gun turret's circular hatch was just above them. 'I need you to cut us a way out! Aim at the roof and give it all you've got!'

There was a rather nervous 'OK' in reply, followed

by a long burst of laser fire. Falling fragments of the hangar's massive stone roof doors came thundering down on top of the ship's hull.

As the rain of rubble subsided, Lorton looked up through the control cabin's transparent canopy. He could see a patch of sky through the gash Beth had blown in the hangar's sealed doors.

Another blast from the Agent's weapons rocked the ship.

'Right,' said the Doctor purposefully, clutching a control column in either hand. 'I think it's safe to say we've outstayed our welcome. Time for a swift exit.'

He pulled back on both columns. Lorton clutched at the console beside him as the ship swung wildly into the air, bucking like a rodeo horse.

'Or any sort of an exit,' muttered the Doctor, reaching for the main throttle.

An instant later, Lorton was sent sprawling as the ship shot like a bullet through the ragged opening in the hangar doors, into the clear sky beyond.

A New Beginning

It had taken the best part of a day to turn the village around. The battered traction tugs that hauled the floating platforms were ancient, and agonisingly slow. Getting them to complete the wide arc necessary to set the village moving back in the direction it had come from had taken an age. Then each and every canopy had needed realigning, to deflect the deadly glare of the suns.

But the villagers had done it. And at long last, they were heading back towards the Dark Cathedral to reclaim their children.

Fra' Vallir stood on the foremost platform, looking eagerly ahead.

After the Doctor had set out for the Cathedral, Vallir had given the stranger's words a great deal of thought. He had been right, of course. Vallir could see now that the so-called Dreamspinner had played him and the other villagers for fools.

But we were bewitched. Bewitched into giving up our own children.

Since the woman had left the village, it had felt as though a fog had slowly lifted from Vallir's mind. The sluggishness that had prevented him from resisting her had passed.

It hadn't taken him long to persuade the other councillors that they had made a terrible mistake – that whatever the consequences might be for standing up to a friend of the Darksmiths, they could not be more terrible than the loss and shame they all now felt.

I only hope we're not too late to put things right…

Out of the corner of his eye, Vallir caught a movement in the sky up ahead. A rock spoorl probably. He squinted against the glare of the suns. Yes, there it was. A dark dot moving across the sky. Moving quickly…

Vallir watched in astonishment as the dark speck grew rapidly. This was no flying beast. As it approached at amazing speed, its form became clearer. It was a winged vessel, a flying craft of a sort Vallir had never seen before.

The machine swooped low over the village canopies. The roar of its engines caused many other villagers to rush from their cabins. They gaped in open-mouthed amazement as the craft looped around to approach again, more steadily.

The ship slowed to a hover, then settled gently on the dusty terrain. The roar of its engines died to a gentle whine.

Vallir watched, pulse racing, as a hatch in the strange craft's side hissed open to form an access ramp. *Is this some device of the Darksmiths?* he wondered anxiously. *Are we to face them so soon?*

But it was a familiar suited figure that came striding cheerfully down the ramp. And at his side, dishevelled but triumphant-looking, were young Lorton and Bethin, with whose grandfather Vallir had so recently made peace.

The Doctor gave a friendly salute. 'Good to see you again, Mr Vallir!' He beamed up at the bewildered Chief Councillor. 'I think we have something on board that belongs to you…'

And bursting from the spaceship's hatch behind him, yelling excitedly to their parents as they streamed down the access ramp, came a mob of bedraggled children, led by Vallir's own son.

Less than an hour later, Lorton and Bethin stood inside the TARDIS, gaping at its mind-boggling interior.

Once the flurry of thanks and questions following his return with the village children had died down, the Doctor had wasted little time getting back to his craft. He was keen to see the Eternity Crystal safely stowed in the stasis box and back inside the TARDIS once again. It had seemed only fair to let his new friends come along to take a look around.

'There!' he said, closing the stasis box. 'Safely out of harm's way again. Now then…'

He crossed to the main console, and fired up one of the system displays. As his fingers flew lightly across the console, the data he had uploaded to the TARDIS systems scrolled across the screen.

'Either of you two any good at puzzles?' he asked, frowning at the display.

As Lorton and Bethin joined him, he gestured to the screen.

'This is stuff from the journal I found in the Dark Cathedral library. But it's incomplete. Old Varlos clearly decided to abandon his "Eternity Device" project – whatever that is. He must have fled the

Collective. If I'm going to find out how to put the Crystal out of action permanently, I need to track him down.'

He froze the display, and gestured for them to take a look.

'This was the last page he wrote. See the scribbled bit in the bottom corner? Some bizarre symbols, and four six-digit numbers arranged around a cross. I thought it might be a clue of some kind.'

Bethin peered at the line of script. 'That's Lithic,' she said quietly. 'It's a sequence of letters and numbers.' She hesitated. 'F… then S… then a five, two zeros, an E, a one and a nine.'

The Doctor scribbled as she spoke, then gave a triumphant whoop. 'Of course! You're a genius! It's a Fijavan Survey code!'

Both children looked at him blankly.

'A location reference,' explained the Doctor. 'The Fijavas were cartographers – map-makers. They dedicated their lives to plotting the positions of the known galaxies.' He was hastily tapping on a keypad as he spoke. 'Their Survey was the first attempt to map the universe. They divided it into sectors. Each one was defined by a simple code, beginning with 'FS'. Here we go…'

A grid-lined star map had appeared on a second display screen.

'...Sector FS500E19.'

The Doctor looked back at the last page from Varlos' journal and pointed to the rough sketch of the numbered cross.

'These six-digit numbers are the grid references. And the cross is telling us to plot lines from this point to this point, and from this one to this one! I'll bet my hat that where the lines cross is where Varlos was heading!'

He tapped at the keyboard again, and the two halves of the puzzle were combined on a single screen.

Activity

Plot lines to locate Varlos' destination.

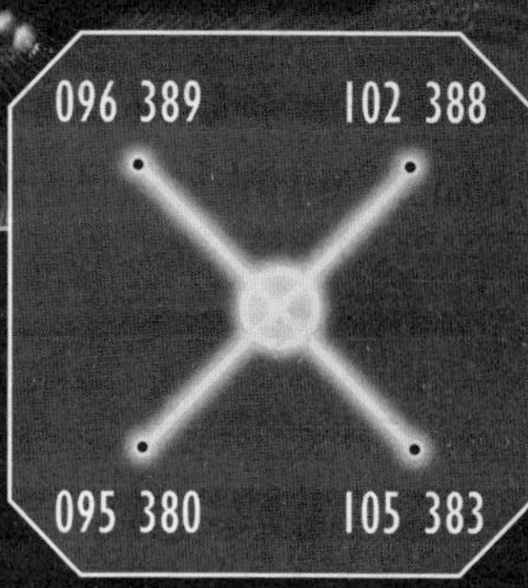

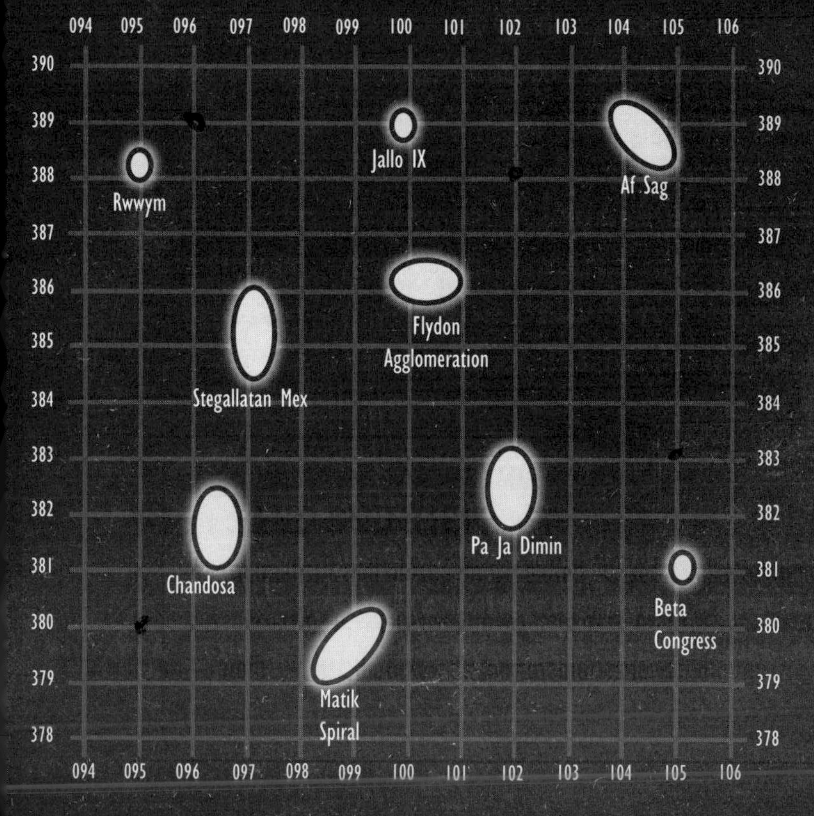

'Right!' The Doctor clapped his hands. 'Well, now I know where I'm headed...' He turned to Lorton and Bethin with a resigned look. '...I really ought to be going.'

Both children looked down glumly. The Doctor wrapped an arm warmly around each of them.

'And you two had better go check on your granddad,' he said, as he escorted them down the ramp to the TARDIS doors. 'Don't want him getting locked up again, do we?'

Lorton managed a grin.

At the doorway, the Doctor paused. 'There should be enough advanced equipment and materials in Shas-Raklat's ship to give your village a major technological leg-up. You won't have to skulk around for Darksmith leftovers any more.'

He bent to give each child a final brief hug, then straightened. 'Now – scram!'

As the double doors closed, the Doctor stared thoughtfully at them for a moment. Then he bounded back up the ramp to the console, and began frantically programming the navigation system with the new co-ordinates.

He checked on the screen, where the solution to the puzzle Varlos had left in his diary was now displayed. The Doctor's destination, the Flydon Agglomeration, covered a big area of space, but right at the co-ordinates Varlos had hidden in his puzzle was the planet Flydon Maxima.

The Doctor knew that the planet was known by another name as well, but it didn't put him off. 'Right then, Flydon Maxima – brace yourself…'

He threw a final lever, and the TARDIS started on its journey through space to the planet known as Despair.

'… because here I come!'

'The fool!' spat High Minister Drakon, watching the small glowing blip move steadily across the scanner screen. 'He seeks to escape us – believes himself to have succeeded in stealing the Eternity Crystal from us!'

He gave a dry, callous bark that was as close to a laugh as his kind could muster.

'Now that our scanners are keyed to the Crystal itself, it will be child's play to track his course, for all the cleverness of his ship's shielding systems.'

Drakon looked up from the scanner to address the other Witan ministers gathered around him. 'This is most satisfactory. To fulfil our contract, we must deliver the Device to our client fully operational. Only the traitor Varlos knows how the Crystal is integrated in its workings. And now this meddlesome Doctor will track him down on our behalf. All *we* need do is follow!'

A figure in a brown cloak stepped forward, somewhat nervously. 'With due respect, High Minister, our Agent's analysis of his physical make-up suggests this Doctor could be a Time Lord. What if his vessel can indeed travel the Space-Time Vortex? Might he not hide, or seek Varlos, in a past or future time – somewhere we *can't* follow?'

'Have faith, Brother Stemnos.' It was Sister Hellan, robed in deep purple, who now spoke. 'There is nowhere the Doctor can hide. Brother Ardos and Sister Clathine have been working on the Agent since its recovery. They assure me that in its latest configuration, its space-time-travel capabilities are greater than ever. It is unstoppable. And even now, Ardos is supervising its dispatch. It will pursue the Doctor mercilessly – through space *or* time.'

Another Witan member, in a cloak of emerald green, stepped forward – Brother Krazon, Minister for Justice.

'I share Sister Hellan's confidence in Ardos' magnificent creation, High Minister,' rasped Krazon. 'Nevertheless, there is a possible contingency plan, in case Varlos or the Time Lord should evade our Agent once more.'

'Go on.'

'In the eyes of intergalactic law, the Doctor's removal of the Crystal, in the full knowledge of its rightful ownership by our Collective, constitutes common theft. And under Clause 374 of the Shadow Proclamation, "theft of an artefact of great cultural value legitimises the use of lethal force to ensure the artefact's recovery".'

High Minister Drakon's thin, colourless lips spread in a cruel sneer. 'Are you saying...'

'Yes, High Minister. We can lawfully set our Dreadbringers in pursuit of the Doctor.'

Drakon's eyes flared with malevolent passion. 'Do it, Krazon! I want the Dreadnought *Adamantine* space-worthy within the hour, carrying a full battalion of your finest soldiers.'

Brother Krazon nodded smartly, and hurried away.

Drakon looked back at the glowing blip on the scanner screen, slowly moving away from its centre, and gave another dry cackle. 'That's right, Doctor

– run! Run as fast as you can. For, by stone and sun-fire, you have incurred the wrath of the Darksmiths of Karagula – and now your very nightmares are coming after you!'

To Be Continued...

To find out what events lie in store for the Doctor and the mystery of the Darksmith Legacy, look out for The Depths of Despair.

But for now, here is a taste of things to come...

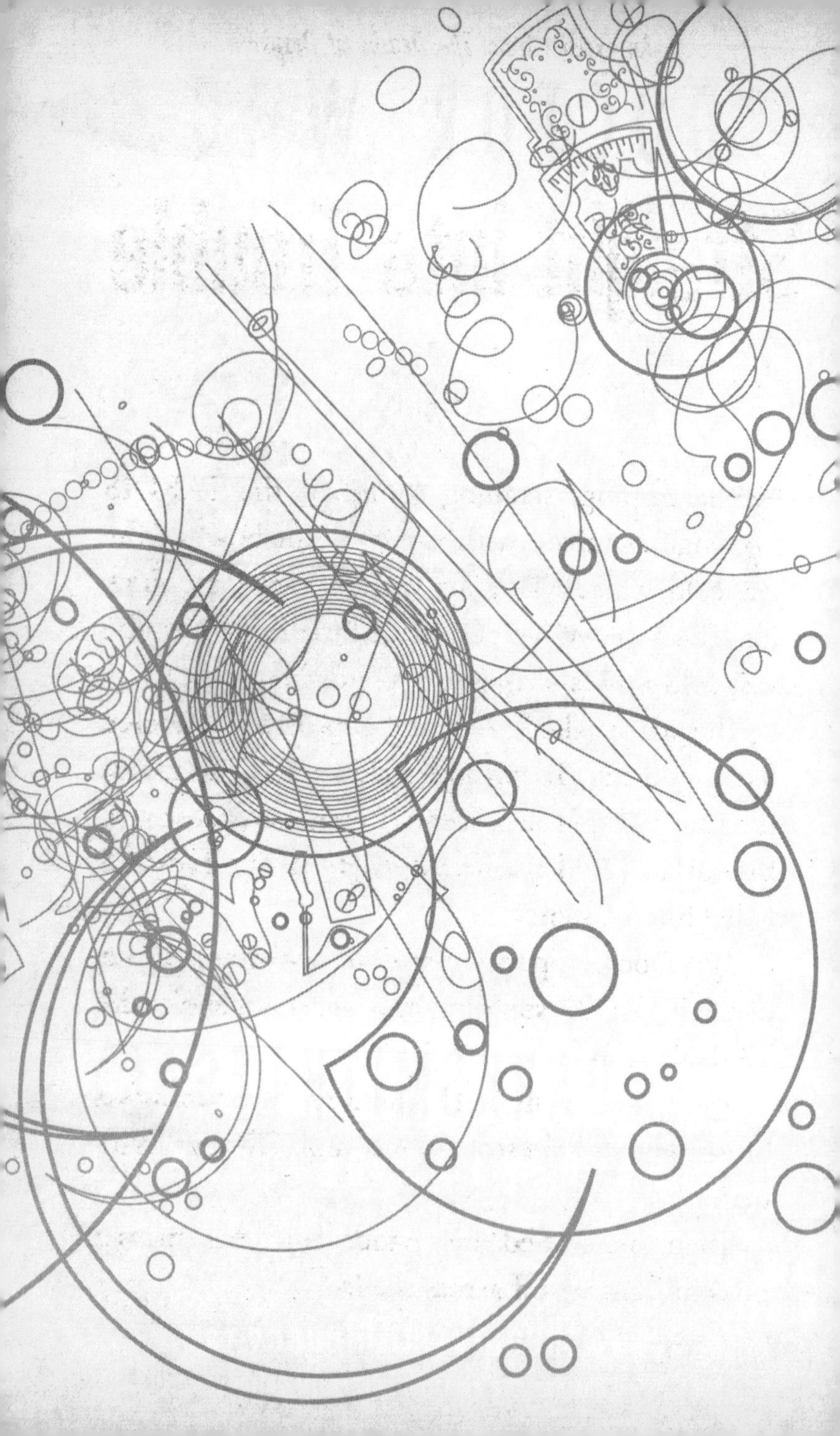

An excerpt from *The Depths of Despair*

Straight into Trouble

The rasping, scraping sound of the TARDIS engines mixed with the constant howl of the cold wind. Misty air swirled above the thick ice. The weak yellow sun made little impact on the vast cold wastes of the planet's northern pole.

The ice creaked. A crack appeared – sudden, like a gunshot. It spread quickly across the ice, as if a heavy weight had been dropped abruptly on to the surface. And the heavy weight of the TARDIS faded into existence.

The Doctor opened the door and stepped out of the TARDIS, standing at a slight angle like the TARDIS itself.

'Odd,' he murmured to himself. 'Everything's a bit skewwhiff.' He straightened up. 'Oh yes. That's better.'

Then he stuffed his hands into his trouser pockets, and set off across the ice.

DOCTOR · WHO

Fantastic free Doctor Who slipcase offer when you buy two Darksmith Legacy books!

Limited to the first 500 respondents!

To be eligible to receive your free slipcase, fill in your details on the form below and send along with original receipt(s) showing the purchase of two Darksmith Legacy books. The first 500 correctly completed forms will receive a slipcase.

Offer subject to availability. Terms and conditions apply. See overleaf for details.

Entry Form

Name: ....

Address: ....

Email: ....

Have you remembered to include your two original sales receipts? ⬡

I have read and agree to the terms and conditions overleaf. ⬡

Tick here if you don't want to receive marketing communications from Penguin Brands and Licensing. ⬡

Important – Are you over 13 years old?

If you are 13 or over just tick this box, you don't need to do anything else. ⬡

If you are under 13, you must get your parent or guardian to enter the promotion on your behalf. If they agree, please show them the notice below.

Notice to parent/guardian of entrants under 13 years old

If you are a parent/guardian of the entrant and you consent to the retention and use of the entrant's personal details by Penguin Brands and Licensing for the purposes of this promotion, please tick this box. ⬡

Name of parent/guardian: ....

Terms and Conditions

1. This promotion is subject to availability and is limited to the first 500 correctly completed respondents received.
2. This promotion is open to all residents aged 7 years or over in the UK, with the exception of employees of the Promoter, their immediate families and anyone else connected with this promotion. Entries from entrants under the age of 13 years must be made by a parent/guardian on their behalf.
3. The Promoter accepts no responsibility for any entries that are incomplete, illegal or fail to reach the promoter for any reason. Proof of sending is not proof of receipt. Entries via agents or third parties are invalid.
4. Only one entry per person. No entrant may receive more than one slipcase.
5. To enter, fill in your details on the entry form and send along with original sales receipt(s) showing purchase of two Doctor Who: The Darksmith Legacy books to: Doctor Who Slipcase Offer, Brands and Licensing, 80 Strand, London, WC2R 0RL.
6. The first 500 correctly completed entries will receive a slipcase.
7. Offer only available on purchases of Doctor Who: The Darksmith Legacy books.
8. Please allow 31days for receipt of your slip case.
9. Slip cases are subject to availability. In the event of exceptional circumstances, the Promoter reserves the right to amend or foreclose the promotion without notice. No correspondence will be entered into.
10. All instructions given on the entry form, form part of the terms and conditions.
11. The Promoter will use any data submitted by entrants for only the purposes of running the promotion, unless otherwise stated in the entry details. By entering this promotion, all entrants consent to the use of their personal data by the Promoter for the purposes of the administration of this promotion and any other purposes to which the entrant has consented.
12. By entering this promotion, each entrant agrees to be bound by these terms and conditions.
13. The Promoter is Penguin Books Limited, 80 Strand, London WC2R 0RL.

Cut Here

Doctor Who Slipcase Offer
Brands and Licensing
80 Strand
London
WC2R 0RL